NAILED!

An Erotic Death Anthology

EDITED BY

Lyle Perez-Tinics

Charlotte Emma Gledson

Rainstorm Press
PO BOX 391038
Anza, Ca 92539
www.RainstormPress.com

ISBN 10 – 1937758109
ISBN 13 – 978-1-937758-10-3

Library of Congress Control Number: 2012902337

Nailed! An Erotic Death Anthology
Publisher: Rainstorm Press www.RainstormPress.com
Copyright © 2011 by Rainstorm Press
Copyright continues at end of book.
All rights reserved.

Interior book design by –
The Mad Formatter
www.TheMadFormatter.com

Cover Design by April Guadiana
Manson26@yahoo.com

DISCLAIMER

The following stories are not for the faint at heart. They contain graphic scenes of sexual acts and mutilation that some may say is "too much". If you are easily disturbed by such things, please close this book and give it to someone who is not. Enjoy and thank you.

TABLE OF CONTENTS

NAILED!

An Erotic Death Anthology

ANOTHER POV
Matt Kurtz

Even though his business was doing extremely well, Robert Spruceton just couldn't help but feel as if something were missing. The job's excitement seemed to have lost its flare, which was ironic, because most men would have killed to do what he did for a living.

Robert was a professional pornographer.

In an industry that earned seven billion dollars a year, Robert, along with his right-hand man and on-screen talent Dick Herhard, earned their generous slice of the pie with their *Amateur Initiations* line, a niche market that dealt with girls just starting out in the business. Robert handled the business end—having solely financed the endeavor a decade earlier—while Dick was top banana because of his auteur directing style that struck a chord with the fans and turned a sizable profit with each new release.

Although their blowjob series, *Tonsil Attack,* was a bestseller, their full-on fuck flicks weren't doing too shabby either. The location used for all their videos was simple and practical: their living room. This wasn't porn for couples with fancy music and exotic locations. This was reality.

And a harsh one at that.

Dick shot all the videos in the point of view perspective—or as they say in the business, POV—holding the camera himself, becoming a surrogate of pleasure to the viewer at home. Even though he was the on-screen talent, shooting in POV allowed him near anonymity, as he kept his less-than-stellar mug off screen. (Which was just fine, since his true selling point was the almost ten inches of meat that swung between his legs.) As the taping was going on, Robert kept his distance while still maintaining an eye on the production, ensuring that things rolled smoothly for his gifted director.

The women they used for their videos were the fresh-off-the-bus types, found through a low-level modeling agency specializing in the adult entertainment industry. Amateurs were the cheapest and kept the overhead low. They were also so inexperienced with the way the business worked that it allowed Dick to get a little rough with them for no additional fee.

Naivety and innocence. That's what their fans wanted.

They wanted the girl next door.

They wanted reality.

They—especially Dick—wanted fresh meat.

Everything that Dick did on camera, he did while keeping his fans in mind. He was a true showman, always playing it up for the audience. When it came to their fuck series, the fans blogged on their website's forum about how they loved that flicker of pain on the girl's face when Dick penetrated her with his beefy cock.

So Dick gave the fans what they wanted: aim the camera on the girl's face to capture that initial gasp upon penetration, then pan down to his own belly, where her hand would already be planted, holding him back from going in too deep too suddenly. Dick waited for the girl to relax a little, allowing her to think that the worst might be over, and then he'd quickly thrust an inch or two deeper just to make her gasp louder. (And if the girl was a real screamer, he'd give her the whole kabob, thrusting balls-deep for the ultimate in cinematic experience.)

It was a given that Dick had to incorporate the same technique into *Tonsil Attack*. A little unexpected thrust or two on his part always resulted in a hearty gag, snot bubbles, and watery eyes. It proved to the fans that these girls were indeed amateurs, with the only downside being if the chick happened to puke her lunch in his lap.

Witnessing such sickening spectacles made Robert want to

retire from the business altogether while he still had an ounce of humanity left. Only in his late thirties, he had made more than enough money over the past decade to live comfortably, well into his golden years. Envying the common man with his boring existence, Robert hoped that it wasn't too late to settle down, start a family, and put the life he'd made for himself far behind.

Whenever Robert sat back and allowed Dick's sadism to run rampant because it was great for business, the former became as much a monster as the latter. But today, Robert felt hopeful that not all was lost, since he was experiencing a human emotion that had left him years ago: anticipation.

It was all because *she* would be on their doorstep at any moment. Lola Darling (presumably not her real name) had done the unheard of. She bypassed the agency and contacted Robert directly over the phone, letting him know that she wanted to be in one of their videos. She had no interest in the biz other than the mere curiosity of what it would feel like to perform on camera, as she put it, "at least just this once."

Lola had chosen *Tonsil Attack*, guaranteeing that her oral skills would blow away—pun intended—any other job that Dick had received. She was willing to bet that her talent would land her the coveted spot of cover girl on their next DVD release.

Upon hearing this, Dick was hardly impressed; a thousand girls had fed him the same bullshit, trying to build themselves up. But what Dick really didn't like was the fact that Lola refused to e-mail a photo of herself. What if she had a horse face? Or was some fatty? When Robert tactfully brought up Dick's concern to Lola over the phone, she assured him that she had viewed numerous videos released by Dick Herhard Productions and was quite confident that her ample good looks fit the bill.

It was still too fishy for Dick. There had to be a catch in there somewhere.

It wasn't until he was informed of Lola's asking price that he finally warmed up to the proposition. Lola was willing to do it for *free*. No backend deal, no percentage of profits. Just a free blow like it was from your own girlfriend … while filming it, of course.

Robert thought that maybe she was some sort of groupie. Or maybe she was doing it to get back at a boyfriend, hubby, or daddy.

Dick couldn't give two shits about the reason. All he knew was this was going to be good, because unlike all the others, she *desired* it. For once it wasn't about some whore doing it for a paycheck. At Dick's insistence, Robert called her back to set up a shoot date for the video.

With all this mystery, the wheels were really spinning in Dick's head on how to market her appearance on the DVD cover, especially if she was as orally blessed as she claimed to be. Now since Lola was doing it for free, she was a slut, not a whore. He thought about it a little more. *Lola: The Real Life Nympho! Lola: The Cum-Hungry Pole-Swallower!* He had to laugh at that one, because it was reminiscent of those tacky sideshow banners for the traveling circus he'd seen as a kid. The more he thought about it, the more he liked the circus angle. Who said smut couldn't be creative?

Robert was setting up the final light in the living room when the doorbell rang.

"This bitch better suck like a goddamn Hoover," Dick grumbled.

Robert nodded, stepping aside so that Dick could greet the mysterious woman on their doorstep. Horse face or not, the talent had arrived. It was time for Robert to go into wallflower mode.

Dick opened the door, revealing an attractive woman standing on the porch. She appeared to be in her late twenties or earlier thirties—a lot older than what they were used to dealing with, and something she had failed to mention over the phone.

Because of her age, Dick almost slammed the door in her face. But his curiosity about the woman got the best of him. He gave her the once over. *Hmmmmm. Tight body. Pretty face. Nice tits. Definitely old enough to have shit out a kid or two. Well? How about ... Lola: The Cum Hungry MILF! It's Mommy's Turn for the Milk!*

Though Dick was satisfied with the woman's looks—with all the young things his cock had been shoved into, he couldn't help but be a little jaded—Robert couldn't believe Lola's beauty. Even with hardly any makeup on, she was gorgeous enough to be what he considered 'wife material.' Just a nice, wholesome, natural look that was way more beautiful than any skank her age still in the business.

After the front door closed behind her, Lola smiled and held up a duffle bag. "Brought a couple outfits. I want you to pick out your favorite."

Dick liked that she already knew who was in charge.

Robert just liked that incredible smile.

"Sounds good," Dick said. "I'll show you to the bathroom so you can freshen up and try a couple on."

Robert was tweaking the lights when she walked out wearing a silk robe that barely covered her ass cheeks. With her tan muscular legs, Dick was a little disappointed that she had only agreed to a blowjob video. *Geez. Those great legs spread wide in the air—or hell, propped over my shoulders—with me pounding away at her ... that shit would look poetic on camera.*

"You like it?" she asked, spinning around. The movement lifted the flimsy garment, allowing a peek at a black thong that was wedged between two ass cheeks just as incredible as her legs.

"Yes, very much," Dick said with a smile.

"Okay, take a mental note on this one. I'll go try on another."

"No. Forget it. That one's fine." Though he was sure

Robert wanted to see more, Dick was already getting hard, craving something more than a stupid fashion show.

Lola giggled. "That was easy enough." After an uncomfortable beat, she shrugged. "So? Now what?"

"Let's get all the waivers and releases signed. You brought the results from your HIV screening, right?"

"It's in my bag."

"Go get it so we can make a copy for our records. Oh, and your driver's license, too. Need a copy of that to prove you're legal."

She shot him a sarcastic look. "C'mon, don't I look over eighteen?"

You look beautiful, Robert thought, grinning like the village idiot.

"Doesn't matter what I think," Dick said. "It's for the records that we gotta keep in order to stay outta jail."

As Dick stepped back to go over any last-minute details of the shoot, Lola retrieved her bag and went to the kitchen table, Robert following close behind. She handed him her test results and driver's license.

He paused, looking down at them. "Uh-oh."

Lola glanced up.

Robert held up the driver's license, a flimsy piece of paper with no picture on it. "This is a temporary."

"My purse got stolen last week. That's all I got." She giggled nervously. "I swear it's legit."

Robert stepped around the table, shielding Lola from Dick to keep their conversation private. The last thing he needed now was for Dick to go all ballistic on them. In a low voice, he whispered, "I'm sure it's legit, but we need legal documentation. Something with a photo on it. Do you have anything else?"

"I just told you that my purse was stolen. Every ID I had was in my wallet. Which was in my purse."

"I know, but-"

"Look, I could see this being a hassle if I were trying to buy a plane ticket. But if a photoless document is good enough to legally drive a car, it should be good enough to suck some guy off on camera in his own living room. Right?"

Robert winced a little at her frankness. For just a moment, he was caught up in an ordinary conversation with an extraordinarily beautiful woman, completely forgetting what she was really here to do.

"Okay," she said. "This is all about trying to prove that I'm of legal age, right? Well, I'm flattered that you could possibly question that but ... c'mon, I'm thirty-one years old."

"But it's just that-"

Lola pushed her chair back and reached for her bag.

"Wait!" Robert pleaded, then realized how loud he'd spoken. He glanced over his shoulder and lowered his volume. "It's fine. You're right. I'm just being a stickler. Please stay." Robert really didn't want her to leave, not yet. Dick would never know about the temporary, because Robert was the one who handled the paperwork.

Fuck it. Any blind man could see that she was well beyond the legal age. She was a woman.

A *real* woman.

Robert winked at her. "I'll go make the copies. You fill out the releases, okay?"

Lola nodded, flashed him her gorgeous smile, and scooted closer to the documents on the kitchen table.

"Be right back," he said.

When Robert left to make the necessary copies, Lola glanced over the paperwork that would allow Dick Herhard Productions to do whatever they wanted with her likeness, whether in photograph, video, audio, Internet stream or any future medium—known or unknown—for the total sum of zero dollars, agreed upon in exchange.

As she signed her name and dated the contract, Robert came back into the room. She glanced up from the paperwork, and when those big brown eyes locked with Robert's, his heart skipped a beat. *God, she's so incredible.* Shifting into business mode, Robert exchanged items with her, and took a few steps back, knowing Dick's policy of limiting interaction with the talent.

"All done," she said. With a playful glance to the living room, she added, "Now, shall we get down to the real business at hand?"

Ah, that was Dick's cue. He strutted over to the equipment bag on the floor for his camera. By the time he stood back up, his pants were already unbuckled.

No goddamn couth, whatsoever, Robert thought, fighting back his disgust.

Lola dug in her bag and pulled out two items. She approached Dick, who was strategically positioning the loveseat dead center of the three-light setup, and offered them up for his approval.

Dick inspected the items: a long piece of black fabric that looked like a blindfold, and a shiny, silver vibrator.

"You ain't gonna need those, honey, not for what we agreed upon," he told her as his pants dropped to his ankles, unleashing his large erection. He spit in his hand and rubbed the head of his cock with the impromptu lubrication in order to keep himself rock hard.

Lola acknowledged how well endowed he was with a whistle, feeding his ego in the process. "On the contrary. Unless you pay me, I can do this however I choose."

Robert winced a little, wondering if there would be an argument. He knew how much Dick hated being contradicted.

Glancing at the fabric, Dick shot her a condescending look. "Use your brain. If ya blindfold me, how the fuck am I gonna be able to film anything?"

"It's not for you. It's for me."

"Our viewers like eye contact. How are they goin' get that with you wearing a stupid blindfold?"

Lola raised the cloth, wrapping it around her head. It wasn't a blindfold, but a mask—one that extended from the top of her forehead to the tip of her nose.

Robert leaned in a little closer. He saw those gorgeous brown eyes highlighted even more by the surrounding void of black.

Dick noticed that the mask still allowed the necessary eye contact, and—more importantly—didn't impede anything going into her mouth. And that was good enough for him. Maybe that circus angle for the DVD could be changed to a Halloween angle. *Lola: The Blowjob Bank Robber! Stealing Semen, Not C-notes!* Dick shrugged. Kinda corny, but it might work. He'd have to bounce it off Robert later to see if it was a keeper.

"And as for this," Lola said, holding up the silver vibrator, "though I get immense pleasure from giving head, this'll take me over the edge, making my performance all the more memorable."

"Again, lady, this ain't some solo masturbation flick. It's nothin' but blowjobs."

"I only need my mouth and one hand to take care of you. Trust me; it'll be a very short scene if I use my two-handed technique. So my other hand is free to do as I choose." She held up the vibrator again. "And this is what I choose to do with it."

Dick shook his head. "Ain't gonna happen. The camera mic will pick up the vibrating between your legs and make it sound like you got a swarm of flies infesting your snatch."

"Fine, then I won't turn it on. Okay?"

Robert watched as Lola kept her eyes locked with Dick's, waiting for his response. This woman wasn't like all the others. She had strength, a self-assured power, which made her even more attractive to Robert. Why couldn't he have met her in any other goddamn situation?

Dick liked the fact that the releases had already been signed. Once the camera started recording, this bitch was going to be in his world. *We'll see how strong she is then*, Dick thought. He just hoped that after a good thrust, her tears would still read on camera, with her wearing that dumb mask and all.

"Fine," he said. "Whatever." Dick stepped out of the pants bunched up around his ankles and sat on the loveseat. He spat in his hand again for the extra lube.

Lola turned to the mirror hanging on the living room wall. She adjusted her mask in its reflection, making sure it was snug and secure.

Robert took a step back, watching Lola from the distance with butterflies flapping against the walls of his stomach. Was he really going to let this happen?

"Kneel down in front of me," Dick told her. "I've gotta check my focus."

Lola did as commanded. She playfully ran her long finger-nails over his naked thighs. Her forearm brushed against his erection, causing his cock to bounce from the sensation of her soft skin.

"Well, hello there," she purred.

"Save it for when we're rollin'," he said, studying the LCD flip-screen on the camera. "Look up at me." When she did, he rotated a dial. "Okay, good." And it did look good, especially those eyes looking up at him through the mask. The woman obviously had an artistic streak. Dick lowered the camera to his side. "Okay, here's what's gonna happen. I need you to stand in the middle of the—"

"Oh, wait!" Lola shouted in excitement. She sprang up and pranced to the middle of the living room. "I told you that I've seen all your videos. You always start off by saying, 'And who do we have here?'" The last words were said in a mockingly deep voice.

Robert almost laughed at her amusing imitation of Dick.

She continued, with a shit-eating grin. "Then I state my name, age, and where I'm from. Right?"

Dick didn't find any of this even remotely cute. "Ah, yeah. When I start recording, I'll ask ya that and you give the answers. Then ya drop your robe and —"

"I'll drop it when I feel that the time is right."

"You'll drop it and show your goddamn tits after your introduction! That's how it's done!"

She held up her hand for him to relax. "Duly noted. But don't you think it's sexier if I keep it on for a bit? It'll build up the anticipation. Like foreplay. The way I see it, we're already working this mysterious angle with the mask thing, so how about we tease the audience until they're practically screaming at their television sets for me to remove the robe?"

Robert wanted to scream, "God, this girl is good! Listen to her, Dick, ya asshole!" But he knew better.

Dick eyed her up and down for a moment and cracked a smug smile. "You've put some thought into this, haven't you?"

She nodded, winked, and cast a grin.

Yeah, keep it up bitch. We'll see how much you're smiling when I give you the Dick Herhard extra thrust to your tonsils. "Fine. Let's just get rollin'."

Dick hit the REC button on the camera, aimed it at Lola, and counted silently to ten for plenty of pre-roll on the tape.

One…

Two…

Three…

Robert's heart started to flutter. This was it. Was he really going to just sit back and allow Dick to destroy this woman, who finally made him feel something inside again? *Could* he let that happen? He wanted to call out for them to stop. Tell them that all bets were off. That this was all one big mistake.

But instead, he remained silent. The camera was rolling. Dick was in charge now.

Four…

Five…

Six...

Lola stared at Dick through the mask. Tightly clutching the vibrator, she gave the place the once-over and saw that the blinds were closed for their privacy. She looked at the lighting setup, the make and model of Dick's camera, and realized the video they were about to make was going to be one of high quality. Taking a deep breath, she waited for his cue.

Seven...

Eight...

Nine...

Dick glared at Lola as she stood in the middle of the living room. He waited for that hesitation (possibly fear) in her eyes. But she appeared completely relaxed. *Too* relaxed, in fact. Maybe it was because of the mask. It covered enough of her face to give her almost complete anonymity. Well, whatever it was, she better be as good as she claimed to be.

Ten...

"And who do we have here?"

After her brief introduction, Lola knelt before him. When she started her performance, Dick almost shuddered at how extraordinary it was. The woman knew her way around a cock, just like she said. His bare feet slowly rubbed back and forth across the plush carpet, adding to the already incredible sensation he was feeling all over. Any of her bullshit up to this point was quickly forgotten in the face of her mind-boggling skill.

There was no direction he could possibly give to enhance her already perfected technique. He didn't know how much longer he'd be able to last. Forget baseball stats or his Grandma in a bathing suit! Instead, he tried to keep from popping by thinking of some incentive to offer Lola to get her back for additional videos. He knew his fans would request more. And he was all about pleasing the fans.

Robert looked away from the performance. He should have stopped it before it even began. She might have been The

One. She already seemed accepting of what he did for a living, something he knew would be a major deal breaker with most women. But now it was too late.

She was just like all the others who came and went from this living room.

Tainted.

In between her animalistic grunts and head bobbing, Lola tightly squeezed the vibrator in her free hand. Then she stopped abruptly and looked up at Dick.

Dick wanted to yell, "What in God's name did you stop for!" But what came out instead was an incoherent babble.

Robert looked over at Lola to see if there was a problem.

"Keep it rolling," Lola said, then reached for Dick's camera.

He pulled it away from her like a child not willing to share his toy, only wanting that heavenly mouth wrapped around his cock again.

"Why … why did you stop?" he finally sputtered.

Lola glanced at the solid red light on the front of the camera. "The look on your face, it's … priceless." She couldn't help but giggle. "I told you I was good, didn't I? Now let me film your face."

"No … no, I don't … I never show it onscreen."

"You edit your own movies, right?"

"Yeah."

"Then just edit this part out. But I guarantee you'll get a big kick out of seeing the smile I'm putting on your face in the editing room later." She reached for the camera again and teased, "C'mon. Or I won't let you do exactly *that* to my face."

Dick shoved the camera in her hand.

Lola zoomed in and out on his flustered face and held it there in a nice close-up. "This *is* priceless."

Dick chuckled while reaching for the camera.

Lola pulled it away. "You ready for the big finale?"

Dick nodded like a little boy.

"Say it!" she commanded, while making sure that he was center frame on the LCD screen. "Say you want me to finish you off!"

Robert was startled by the shift in the woman's demeanor. What was once perky and playful turned sinister. He had to confess that it drew him in even more. She was indeed a natural born performer.

Dick realized that maybe it wasn't so bad being the submissive one every once in a while. At least to this Lola chick. Besides, like she said, he could always edit this part out. "Yes. Please. Please finish me off."

Lola's attitude softened completely as she returned the camera. She waited until she was confident he had her framed perfectly. "How's your focus?"

"Good," he huffed. "It's all good, beautiful." He leaned back, waiting for his big finale (to come).

Though she was tainted, Robert still felt the bubbling of jealousy from the softer tone Dick was taking with the woman. He'd never seen this side of Dick before.

"Okay, babe," she purred. "Allow me."

Lola twisted the base of the silver vibrator. The top fell off and dropped to the floor. In her hand was a straight razor, unsheathed from the hollow tube.

Oblivious to anything happening beyond the camera's tiny flip screen, Dick didn't see the razor flip open.

Robert opened his mouth to scream a warning, but nothing sounded.

Lola shoved the blade under Dick's chin. He felt the cold steel against his throat and knew something had gone terribly wrong. Still recording, he lowered the camera very slowly, terrified to make any sudden movements.

With her free hand, Lola guided the camera back up so he could maintain her close-up. "Keep rolling, baby."

Both Dick and Robert watched, frozen with fear, as Lola blew a kiss into the lens.

ANOTHER POV

She pushed the blade in and slid it across Dick's neck. Warm blood splashed down his chest, across his belly, and into his naked crotch. Gasping, he dropped the camera and clutched his throat.

Robert wanted to lunge at Lola, but his legs refused to budge. Paralyzed in horror at what this beautiful creature had done, he couldn't make a move to stop her.

Lola snatched the camera and turned it around on Dick, making him the star of the show now. With every beat of his racing heart, blood pumped beneath his hands wrapped around his neck in a futile attempt to stop the precious life from leaking out.

Never taking the camera off Dick, Lola propped it up on the coffee table. She framed a wide shot of the bleeding Dick Herhard spilling all over his loveseat.

Lola tightened the mask across her eyes to make sure her anonymity wasn't compromised. As she did so, she glanced around the place and noted all of the flammable stuff. Once she retrieved the copies of her paperwork with her bogus signature and equally fake temporary ID, she'd wipe her fingerprints off the few things she had touched, then finish the cleansing with a single match and the gas cans sitting in the trunk of her car.

But right now, she had other pertinent matters at hand — namely that lump on the loveseat bleeding like a stuck pig. She was going to have to work quickly. The severity of the wound was only going to allow her a minute or two — tops — before he expired.

And that's when things were really going to get messy.

Because that's what happened on the videos that *she* produced.

She was about to become an even richer woman. Having to blow this piece of shit at her wealthy client's request made her charge extra.

A lot extra.

But that's what her client wanted. And she was all about pleasing them. She dominated a select niche of the snuff market known as the point-of-view killing, where the viewer was the one murdered. The camera became the surrogate of slaughter for the viewer at home.

Clients with more money than God were paying through the roof for it, feverishly outbidding one another on the black market because of its limited quantity.

It was a risky business. But well worth the rewards.

Her days of butchering and dissecting some drugged-up runaway on film were far behind her. In fact, she had just outdone herself, rising above the niche she had already dominated. Besides blowing the victim, along with a kiss into the camera, her client had specifically requested some sort of celebrity snuff.

And she had delivered one.

Sure, a minor celebrity—at least in some circles—but still a celebrity all the same. She had to start somewhere, right?

So with her client's approval, Lola had delivered up one pornographer Robert Spruceton—who also went by the stage name of Dick Herhard—as the first of many in her *Celebrity Victims* line of DVDs.

FUCKING REVENGE
Nelia Thompson

Hand in hand the couple walked into the hotel room.

Julia bit her lip and hung back slightly.

Eddie could tell she was nervous. Gently, he tugged her forward, sitting on the edge of the bed, with her standing in front of him.

She looked down shyly, her long dark hair falling forward to cover half of her face.

"Hey, look at me," he said softly.

She glanced up and her dark brown eyes flicked over his face before darting away again.

He brushed her hair back and cupped her face, making her look directly at him. What he saw in her eyes confused him – he saw uncertainty and nervousness.

"I thought you wanted this," he said. "I thought you wanted *me*."

"Oh, I do," she hurriedly reassured him, placing her hands over his; she closed her eyes and pressed her cheek into his palm.

"Then what's wrong?"

She sighed heavily, opening her eyes, looking at him briefly before looking down again.

"I'm just a little nervous," she said, "I've only ever been with one man, and I don't want to disappoint you."

He froze, thinking: Why hasn't she told me this before? Is she scared? "I'm not going to hurt you," he said, lifting her chin gently.

"I know," she giggled.

"If you don't want to, or you're unsure, we don't have to do this now," he said, searching her face for any signs of fear.

Julia shook her head and bit her bottom lip. "No, I want

to."

Eddie took both of her hands in his. "If you're sure …"

"I'm sure," she said and giggled again.

He could see she was relaxing – her vibrant personality was beginning to shine through again. He smiled encouragingly.

She bit her lip again, then grinned."Close your eyes," she commanded softly.

He grinned; he loved it when she was playful. Closing his eyes he waited to see what she was going to do. He felt her withdrawing her hands from his and let her go. He felt her small soft hands on his face – one on either side of his jaw.

She tilted his head back.

He let her. Eddie felt her brush her lips against his in slow, soft, little kisses, flicking her tongue lightly against his lips with each one; she moved back and forth from one corner of his mouth to the other, and it took all of his strength of will not to grab her and pull her closer.

The little teasing kisses stopped.

Eddie opened his eyes and looked at her; she was no longer shy and all of her timidness had vanished. He watched her as she reached forward and tugged at his shirt, trying to take it off; he helped her.

Julia stepped back and grabbed the hem of her blouse, grinning. "Gotta keep things fair," she teased, and slipped her top over her head, revealing a black see-through bra.

He groaned.

She smiled.

Julia moved around the side of the bed and climbed on to kneel behind him. She kissed the back of his neck softly, letting her lips skim across his skin. She placed just the tips of her fingers on either side of his neck, sliding them over the tops of his shoulders, down the backs of his arms, and slowly back up again. When her fingers made it back to his neck, she slid them down his back – slowly and torturously. When she reached his lower back, she bent down and ran the tip of her tongue up his spine as her fingers danced back to his shoulders.

She scraped her teeth against his shoulder blades, flicking her tongue against his skin, while she moved her hands half way down his back and let them circle around to his stomach.

He held himself still for her tickling, enjoying her playfulness and exploring hands.

She slowly dragged her fingers down his stomach, getting closer and closer to the waist band of his pants. Pausing there, she tickled just above his waist band out to his hips and then back toward his navel. She slowly moved her hands lower, running her fingers over his crotch, lightly teasing.

He groaned and moved his hips to increase the pressure against her hand.

She caressed him for a few moments before withdrawing her hands all together. She got off the bed and stepped back in front of him.

He reached out for her, but she shook her head.

"I'm not done yet," she said with a smile.

He grinned and put his hands on his legs; his palms itched with the need to touch her, but he didn't want to break the spell.

She knelt down and undid his pants.

He watched her, brushing her hair out of her face when it fell forward.

She smiled up at him; when she had his fly undone she stood again. "Stand up," she said.

He stood as she slid his pants down, leaving his underwear.

"Okay," she grinned, "sit back down."

He sat. "Hey, I thought we were keeping this fair," he teased.

She laughed and slid her pants off too, revealing a black thong that matched her bra.

He gripped the edge of the bed and clenched his teeth to keep from touching her.

She knelt, again, on the floor in front of him.

Taking a hold of his ankles, she straightened out his legs until they were supported by the backs of his heels. Bending forward, she swirled the tip of her tongue around the inside bone of his right ankle, then continued up the inside of his leg, flicking her tongue against the back of his knee, before licking up his thigh.

Pausing to give him a wicked grin, she nuzzled toward his crotch. Tilting her head, she scraped her teeth gently along his cock, through his underwear.

He gasped and growled, gripping the edge of bed so hard that his knuckles turned white.

She worked her way to the tip, continuing the sweet torture. Reaching up she hooked her fingers into the top of his underwear, pulling them down just far enough to swirl her tongue around the tip of his erection.

He moaned.

She tugged his underwear down further, taking him into her mouth as far as she could.

He cried out and swore.

She slowly pulled back, letting her lips slide against him, before she journeyed on to give his left leg and ankle the same treatment she'd given the right.

She stood smiling, placing her hands on his shoulders. Leaning down, she ran her tongue along his bottom lip and slid her hands down his arms, gripping his wrists, tugging his hands free from the bed. She brought one hand and then the other to her mouth, licking from the base of his palms to the tips of his middle fingers. She pressed his hands against her breasts. "Touch me," she whispered.

He growled and squeezed her breasts.

She moved her hands back up his arms, taking a little step closer to him, pressing herself into his hands.

He slid his hands around to her back, unhooking her bra. She shivered.

Slipping it off her shoulders, he dropped it onto the floor. Reaching up he cupped her shoulders and brought her closer still; he could feel her warm breasts against him.

He scraped his teeth against her neck, slowly moving lower to her breasts. He teased her nipples – one by one – with his tongue and enjoyed the sound of her breath coming faster in gasping pants.

He released her shoulders, running his hands lightly down her back.

She gasped and arched toward him.

He nipped and scraped his teeth against her nipples until she started whimpering. He moved his hands lower, skimming his fingers over her ass.

She wiggled against him, moaning.

Hooking his thumbs into the sides of her thong, he slowly slid the thin scrap of material off of her. He stood and shed his underwear as well.

They grinned at each other.

Gripping her hips with both hands, he sat on the bed once again, pulling her close to him. Hooking his fingers behind her left knee, he brought her foot up to rest on the edge of the bed, beside him.

Sliding his right hand up to support her lower back, he gripped her ass with the other; bending forward he flicked his tongue lightly against her hot, wet pussy.

She gasped and gripped his shoulders.

Gently and teasingly, he continued to flick his tongue against her. Enjoying how she gasped and shuddered each time; as her hips started to rock with each stroke, he increased the speed and pressure of his tongue.

Her head dropped back and her breath came faster as she shuddered with pleasure.

Eddie moved the hand he had on her ass, and thrust his

thumb inside her, licking her fast and hard.

She cried out as she climaxed, shaking from the intensity of her orgasm.

He supported her quivering body as he continued to lick, thrusting his thumb in and out of her convulsing depths.

Once her spasms subsided, he scooted back further onto the bed, lifting her onto his lap. Pulling her hips down against his, he thrust his hard cock deep inside her as he lay back on the bed.

Julia moaned and rocked against him. "Please, make me please you," she begged.

Holding her hips tight against his, he bucked hard.

She gasped, trying to lift her hips and ride him. "Please," she begged again, whimpering.

He grinned up at her. "You want to please me?"

"Yes!"

"I want you to touch yourself," he said with a wink. "I want you to make yourself come again, while I'm inside you."

She gave him a little crooked smile, sliding her hands down over her breasts, pausing to pinch her nipples, causing her muscles to clench around him. She tried to rock her hips against him, but he held her still; she whimpered in protest, but didn't try to fight him. Closing her eyes and licking her lips she reached down and rubbed a finger against the spot he'd licked only moments before. She gasped as she slowly rubbed herself in small circles, growling in frustration at not being able to move her hips.

He groaned and bucked against her again.

Gasping and whimpering, she rubbed herself harder and faster, arching her back. She continued to pinch and tug at her nipple with her other hand, clenching around him and rocking against him as much as she possibly could.

He watched her, gritting his teeth to stay in control, tightening his grip on her hips to keep himself all the way inside her.

"Please," she begged, trying to rock her hips.

He growled and lifted her a fraction of an inch and then bucked into her again.

She cried out.

He did it again, receiving another cry for his effort.

She started panting, her hips bucking irregularly against her rubbing fingers.

He knew she was getting close. He lifted her up so that only the tip of his cock was inside her, before yanking her back down, hard, while bucking up into her at the same time.

Her eyes flew open and she gasped in shallow ragged breaths, still rubbing.

He lifted her and yanked her down again.

Her back arched and she cried out as another orgasm rocked over her.

Growling, he flipped her onto her back, staying inside her. He pulled both of her hands above her head, holding her wrists in one of his hands, pinning them against the bed. With his other hand he continued to rub her pussy, extending her orgasm while he thrust into her violently.

She moaned and shuddered beneath him, bucking against him, trying to meet his every thrust.

"Tell me you like it when I fuck you," he growled, scraping his teeth against her neck.

"I love it when you fuck me," she whimpered and licked his ear.

He rode her faster, groaning and calling out her name as he came deep inside her.

He rocked his hips against her a few more times.

She wrapped her legs around him, making little mewing noises in her throat, rocking with him.

He collapsed on top of her, breathing hard.

She rubbed her nose against his cheek and whispered, "You were amazing – way better than I ever expected."

He chuckled softly and kissed her shoulder. "You were

pretty amazing yourself." He moved to get off of her, but she tightened her legs to keep him.

"No, don't move," she said kissing him, "you feel good on top of me."

With a chuckle, he gave in. "I didn't want to crush you."

"You're not," she murmured.

Soon Julia fell asleep and Eddie rolled off to lay beside her; he put an arm around her waist and hugged her close to him, rubbing his nose against her shoulder. He too fell asleep.

A phone ringing woke them both. Looking around sleepily, they realized that it wasn't the hotel phone sitting on the night stand beside the bed.

Eddie jumped up from the bed and retrieved his pants. "It's my cell," he said, "go back to sleep."

He hit the 'send' button and said, "Hello." He took the phone with him into the bathroom and shut the door.

* * *

Julia pulled the blanket that was laying at the foot of the bed up over herself. She closed her eyes and snuggled back into her pillow, thinking of what they might do when he came back.

She was lost in a fantasy when Eddie came out of the bathroom. She smiled, opened her eyes and stretched, letting the blanket fall and expose her breasts. She saw him look at her naked torso. But she frowned when he clenched his jaw and looked away, gathering up his clothes.

Julia grabbed the blanket and pulled it up to her chin, sitting up; something cold and heavy settled into the pit of her stomach. "What's going on? Is something wrong?" she asked in a small, unsure voice.

Eddie sat heavily on the end of the bed, almost the very spot where they had shared so much pleasure a short while ago; he half turned his head in her direction and sighed. "I'm sorry, but I have to go."

"Go?" she asked, confused. "Go where?" She watched Eddie's shoulders tense just before he slipped his shirt over his head.

"Who was on the phone?" she asked suspiciously.

He stood, fastening his pants; he didn't acknowledge that he'd heard her.

"It was your wife," she whispered. "Wasn't it? I thought you were getting a divorce? You told me you'd filed for one."

He sighed heavily. "We did file, but after we had a meeting with the attorneys we decided to try and work things out."

Julia stared at him. "So, this was what? A fling to you?" Tears slid down her face as her heart shattered.

"No," he said, "you aren't a fling to me. I was actually hoping we could keep seeing each other. I mean we live close enough, we could arrange something once in awhile."

She didn't reply.

Eddie turned to look at her. "You mean a lot to me. I don't want to lose you. I still plan on getting a divorce; it just isn't feasible right now."

She frowned. "Not feasible? What the hell does that mean? That I'm not worth enough for you to want me to belong to you? You just want me to be your call-girl-mistress!" She was angry now; the hurt he was causing fueled her rage.

"I do think you're worth it," he said, walking around the bed and sitting down beside her. "We have a house and vehicles in both our names. The cost of divorcing her right now would leave me with nothing. Do you want me to come to you with nothing?"

"I don't care about that stuff," she sobbed, "I just want to be with you. I love you."

"I love you, too," he whispered and tried to pull her into his arms.

"I don't believe you," she screamed, pushing him away. "If you really loved me, you wouldn't have fucked me and then

33

told me that you were going to stay married. You used me like a whore!"

"Julia, I didn't mean to hurt you. I wanted you so much – I just couldn't help myself. You're everything I've ever dreamed of and have always wanted. I'll do anything not to lose you."

She sat staring at the wall with sobs shaking her body and tears flowing freely down her cheeks. "Leave," she said in a flat voice.

"What?"

She looked at him. "I said leave. You've already lost me. The only thing left for you to do is leave."

He looked into her eyes, saw the pain he'd cause, and knew that he'd in fact truly lost her. She deserved to have a man who would love her and that could be with her. He realized that he'd just lost more than any house or car could ever be worth. He'd lost the love of the woman who held his heart and always would.

"Please, don't do this," he pleaded around a lump in his throat.

She shrugged, threw off the blanket, got off the bed, and started getting dressed; she didn't look at him.

"What if you're pregnant?" he asked, suddenly realizing they hadn't used protection. "What are you going to do if you're pregnant?"

She paused, then continued to get dressed. "I'll let you know if I'm pregnant," she said stiffly. "I wouldn't try to keep your child from you, no matter what relationship we have." She laughed and finally looked at him. "That would be perfect," she said bitterly, "I would get pregnant and then your wife would know about me. Then she *will* divorce you and you won't have either of us."

She laughed again; it was a bitter laugh that ended in a sob. She viciously wiped the tears from her face with the back of her hand.

"Well, since you won't leave," she said, slipping on her

shoes and grabbing her purse, "I will. Have a great life with your wife." Julia moved swiftly toward the door.

"Wait," Eddie called after her.

She paused and turned, her hand on the door knob.

"I love you," he said, coming towards her. "Please don't go. I'll break it off with her, I promise. Just give me a little more time."

He reached up, cupped her face in his hands, and kissed her lips gently.

"I can't lose you," he whispered. "Please, at least tell me you'll think about waiting for me."

She closed her eyes, squeezing out more tears. "I've waited long enough," she said in a choked voice.

Julia yanked open the door and walked out.

* * *

Eddie stood there staring at the door for a long time. He turned around and looked at the bed where he'd been with Julia just hours ago. He could still feel her skin. He could still remember the way she tasted. He could hear the cries and whimpers she'd made as she'd enjoyed him. She was gone now, all gone, because he'd made the wrong decision; he realized too late that he should have told her up front what was going on with him and his wife.

He sat on the edge of the bed, dropping his head into his hands. He was surprised to find that his face was wet, that he was crying. He laughed hollowly. He knew that this day was the best and worst day of his life – the day he'd loved and lost the woman of his dreams.

His cell phone rang. He looked down at it, hoping it was Julia; it was his wife. He answered. "Yeah, I'll be home soon," he said with false cheerfulness. "What are you making for supper?"

He listened.

"I love you, too," he said, squeezing his eyes shut with the effort not to sob into the phone. "See you soon."

Eddie stood and looked at the bed one last time before he turned and left. Going back to the life he hated, the life and woman that gave him no joy.

* * *

Heather sat in her car, waiting in the hotel parking lot. She watched as the 'little internet hussy' – as she preferred to think of the woman – rush out crying; the grin that spread across her face was pure evil. He must have told her we're staying together, she thought with a laugh. I'm sure my little call while they were in their 'love nest' helped leak out that information.

She watched as the woman climbed into her car and drove away – fast.

Biting her lip, she waited a couple of minutes and then dialed her husband's cell phone number again; he answered on the second ring.

"Hi, honey," she chirped into the phone, "I forgot to ask when you'd be home. Will it be soon?"

She listened to his response and scowled at his cheerful tone of voice. Damn, lying bastard, she thought. I can't believe he can calmly ask me what's for supper!

"Spaghetti," she said, "oh, the pasta is boiling! Gotta go! Love you! See you when you get home!"

She pressed 'end' on her phone, started the engine of her car, and drove away, hurrying home to make the supper she'd just said was already cooking.

While she drove, she thought about the coming evening, and how much fun she was going to have with her *loving* husband.

* * *

FUCKING REVENGE

Eddie arrived at the stylish house he shared with his wife, and as soon as he stepped through the door he breathed deeply the tomato sauce, garlic, and herb aroma that shouted spaghetti; his stomach rumbled with hunger.

Closing the door behind himself, he yelled, "I'm home!" Without waiting for a response, he hung his keys by the door and headed down the hall to the master suite, to take a shower. The sounds of Heather working in the kitchen alerted him to where she was, and he was relieved she didn't rush out to greet him; he wanted to take a shower before facing her.

He stripped quickly once he made it into the bathroom, and in less than a minute, was in the shower, scrubbing at himself vigorously, trying to erase the memory of Julia's touch.

His heart ached painfully in his chest as he thought about her, and what she'd said. More than anything he wanted to cling to the sensations, tastes, and smells of her, but he couldn't. He tried to tell his mind that there was no point in thinking about her; she was gone and he'd lost her because of his own stupidity.

As he was climbing out of the shower, Heather's head popped through the doorway, making him jump.

"Oh, there you are," she said. "Supper's ready."

She smiled and disappeared again.

He took a deep breath to try and calm his racing heart while toweling himself dry. He stepped into their adjoining bedroom and pulled open a drawer, extracting a pair of sweat pants and sliding them on. Heading out into the hall and towards the kitchen, he combed his fingers through his hair, wondering if Julia would be online later, and if she would answer his messages, if he sent any.

As he stepped into the kitchen, he noticed Heather was dumping a pot of spaghetti noodles and boiling water into a colander sitting in the sink. He frowned. He could have sworn she'd said the pasta was boiling when she'd called earlier.

37

With a shrug, he dismissed the thought because he knew he hadn't really been listening to her when he'd spoken with her on the phone.

"Everything smells wonderful," he said, moving up behind her, nuzzling her neck and wrapping his arms around her.

"Mmmmm," she said, snuggling back against him. "Careful you don't burn yourself – the pan is still hot."

He chuckled and moved away. "How was your day?" he asked, getting plates and silverware out in preparation of the meal.

"Not too bad," she said, forcing lightness into her voice. "How was yours?"

"Uneventful," he said, setting the small table they had in the kitchen. "Do you want wine with dinner?"

"No, I have ice tea," she said.

How the fuck can he *be* so damn calm? she fumed silently. Cheating bastard!

"Looks great," Eddie said when she carried the pasta and sauce to the table. He grabbed the small basket of garlic bread she had sitting on the counter and placed it on the table, before seating himself in his usual chair.

"Thank you," Heather said, having seated herself while he retrieved the garlic bread.

They made small talk, and at times didn't speak at all during the meal, and soon it was over.

Eddie headed into the living room to watch TV. Heather loaded the dishes into the dishwasher, as was their normal routine.

* * *

When she was done in the kitchen, Heather headed to the living room; she stood in the doorway and smiled as she thought about what would come next. Walking into the room, she slid

38

her shirt off over her head and dropped it to the floor. She wiggled out of her pants and dropped them too.

Eddie's attention remained on the TV, not realizing she was even in the room. It wasn't until she stepped in front of him and straddled his lap – naked – that he was aware of her presence.

"Wow!" he exclaimed, smiling and looking her over. "This is different."

She giggled and kissed him.

"Take me to bed," she whispered, pulling back and looking into his eyes. "I want you."

Eddie stared into her eyes for a moment, wondering what happened to his 'prim and proper' wife; with a mental shrug, he did what he was told, eager to see where all this was going.

She squealed and laughed as he picked her up with her legs still wrapped around his waist and carried her to their bedroom.

He kissed her and leaned forward to lay her down on the bed, but she shook her head 'no'. She unwrapped her legs and found the soft carpet with her toes.

"I want to try something different," she said, tilting her head to the side and looking up at him coyly.

"Something new?" he asked. "Like what?"

She tucked her fingers into the waistband of his pants and walked backwards, pulling him around to the side of the bed.

"Do you trust me?" she asked and pouted.

He laughed. "We've been married for six years! Or course, I trust you."

She grinned. "Take your pants off and lay down on the bed."

He raised one eyebrow, but slid his sweats off and laid down.

"No," she said, "on your back."

He laughed, shook his head, and rolled off his side onto his back.

She opened a small drawer in the night stand and withdrew a pair of handcuffs.

"Hold up!" he exclaimed, sitting up. "Wait a minute. I'm not sure I'm cool with being handcuffed."

She pouted. "Why not? You said you trusted me! Just imagine how proud Dr. Henshaw will be when we tell him about overcoming our trust *and* intimacy issues when we go for therapy next week."

Eddie eyed the handcuffs warily, but nodded his head and laid back down.

Heather crawled up onto the bed and drew his hands up over his head, cuffing him to the headboard.

"See," she said, sitting back. "They aren't so bad."

He grinned, surprised that he was getting turned on be being tied up. "I guess not," he said.

She leaned down and kissed him, taking his cock in her hand, stroking him the way she knew he liked.

He groaned and arched up into her hand, returning the kiss.

She pulled back and sat up. "I want you so bad," she growled, and straddled him, taking him deep inside her.

He groaned, watching her. She rode him slowly with her eyes closed, licking her lips.

He closed his eyes as well and enjoyed the pleasure coursing through his body; thoughts of Julia filled his mind, and for once, he tried to fight them.

He opened his eyes again, to fill his vision with Heather, and gasped in shock at what he saw.

She had a butcher's knife clasped in one hand.

"What the fuck are you doing with a knife?" he screamed, trying to buck her off.

She wouldn't budge, but ground her hips down on him as he struggled, getting more excited. "I'm going to kill you," she said, shivering with pleasure as her grew closer to her climax.

"What? Why?" he asked, still struggling.

"Because you cheated on me," she said, increasing her pace, fucking him harder. "I know you screwed that little bitch today."

"That's crazy!" he screamed. "There's no one else, just you!"

"Liar!" she screamed and stabbed the knife viciously into his shoulder.

He screamed and his body jerked.

She gasped and closed her eyes briefly, enjoying the jerking of his body beneath hers.

"I've known for a long time," she panted, opening her eyes again. "I've read all the texts in your phone and all your emails."

She ripped out the knife and stabbed his other shoulder, whimpering with pleasure.

Eddie screamed. "Please stop," he begged, "I'll do anything. We broke up! Today I broke up with her! I want to be with you, honest!"

She growled. "I don't believe you!" She ripped the knife out of him again and held it poised over his chest for a moment while she brought herself closer to an orgasm; blood dripped from the blade and spattered on his chest.

"I'm sorry..." he cried, "I'm so, so sorry! Please don't do this!"

"Shut up!" she screamed as she came and sank the knife into his heart simultaneously.

After her body stopped quivering, Heather looked down at her husband and smirked at the fear etched into his still features.

"You deserved that, you bastard," she said, climbing off of him and the bed. With a deep sigh, she reached into the drawer of the night stand and withdrew a candle and a small box of matches; she lit the candle and dropped it on the bed.

"Oops!" she said, and giggled.

She watched the fire as it grew, waiting for it to become

stronger, backing up toward the door. Finally, she darted down the hall, grabbed her cell phone, and called 9-1-1, ranting about how she and her husband had been having kinky sex when a candle fell over onto the bed. She screamed and screamed that he was still tied to the bed.

Grabbing a blanket from the couch, she exited the house as the emergency dispatcher instructed her to.

"He's burning!" she screamed into the phone. "Please hurry! Oh, God, he's burning!"

Standing by the mailbox, wearing nothing but a blanket, she watched her house burn down. She choked on her laughter and hoped the dispatcher thought the sounds she was making were frantic sobs.

She watched as the most important things in her life – her husband and their home – was consumed by the raging fire, and she felt free. Free to live her life the way she wanted. But that would have to wait, she decided. She had one more loose end to tie up. The internet whore would have to die too, but that would wait until another day.

SUCK ME DRY!
Anna M. Lowther

Donna sat at the bar, sipping a Bloody Mary. Her tongue slid over her upper lip, seeking any stray drop. She craned her neck to scan the empty, darkened corners and turned back to the bar. "Well, Rick, looks like it's going to be another slow night."

"I guess so. There's supposed to be a business convention this weekend, though. I've seen a lot of taxis in front of the Sheraton across the street. Maybe some of those schlubs won't want to hang out in the hotel bar with the guys they'll be sitting next to in all those sensitivity classes tomorrow. But anyway, you've always got me to keep you company. Refill?"

"No, not yet. It wouldn't be wise to get intoxicated this early. Bad for business, you know." She reached into her tiny Louie Vuitton bag and pulled out a gold-plated cigarette holder. She placed an ultra-thin cigarillo in the tip and Rick slid over to light it for her. The flame made the deep maroon polish covering her impossibly long fingernails sparkle. He was no expert, but they looked natural to him. The salon ones always had such a thick appearance. He was sure her nails were real. In fact, as far as he could see, nothing about Donna looked fake. She was a true, classic beauty. As perfect as any woman had ever been.

He noticed a huge ring on her right hand. Made of heavy gold, it looked expensive. It was a large round globe, surrounded by a circle of stars made from glittering diamonds. One star stuck out from the rest on a thin strand of gold. It almost looked like a shooting star, the kind you're supposed to wish on. Rick had a lot of wishes where Donna was concerned, but she was clearly out of his league. He knew better than to even ask. At least she brought in the business, and most of them were big tippers who tried to impress her by throwing around their money.

"That's some ring, Donna. Is it a gift from an admirer?" Rick wiped the shiny oak bar with a fresh white towel. "Looks old, like some sort of antique."

"Very good, Rick, most observant of you. As a matter of fact, it's ancient." Donna purred. "You might say it's a family heirloom."

Just then the door opened, letting in a blast of icy wind. The man was well over six-feet tall and his sense of self-importance was obvious. He wore a black suit and a deep red shirt with French cuffs, fitted with gold and onyx cufflinks. In the center of his black silk tie was a small gold pin proclaiming his membership in the Royal Order of Masons. He brushed a few snowflakes from his shoulder and dropped onto the stool next to Donna.

"What can I get for you?" Rick asked. He watched Donna glance at the stranger from under her long, black lashes. She tilted her head and let her glossy red hair fall across her cheek, then tossed it back, exposing her alabaster throat. He'd seen that move before, more times than he could count. He knew it wouldn't be long until the new guy would be right where she wanted him. *Lucky bastard!* Rick thought to himself.

"I'll have a Black Velvet, neat. Looks so good on the lady here, that nothing else really comes to mind." The newcomer took the glass from Rick and raised it in salute to Donna.

She rocked her hips to one side and fluffed her hair. "Oh, this old thing? You like it? I've had it for years, but it is still a favorite. The classics never go out of style." Donna smoothed her hands down her sides, following the deep indent of her waist and sliding slowly over her hips. The velvet dress clung to her like she'd been sewn into it. Her caress raised a glossy sheen on the fabric, outlining her body as if she were backlit. She crossed her legs, high at the thigh, allowing a tiny hint of her black lace panties to peek out.

Rick shivered, remembering how she looked when she had come in tonight. The dress had a deep V-neck which allowed her milk-white cleavage to strain forth, teasing with every movement in the hope a breast might be set free. The dress stopped just below the point where her legs became hips. Legs that go all the way to the top and a dress that teases you with the hope of a peek at her treasures, was a combination worth savoring. He let the image burn into his memory, planning to pull it out later after his shift was done and he was back in his lonely apartment.

"I think the dress is quite stunning but you outshine it by far, lovely lady. Might I ask your name? I'm Geoffrey, by the way." He extended a well-manicured hand toward her, a confident smile on his face.

"I'm Donna. So what brings you to our provincial little town, Geoffrey?" She leaned forward and took his hand, for just the briefest of moments as her breasts promised to fall out - - almost.

Rick noticed the man's quick intake of breath when her delicate, pale fingers brushed his hand. She'd only ever touched Rick once, but he'd never forgotten how her skin had felt. He could still remember the electric sparks that had run up his arm, jolts of power from each fingertip. She was an amazing woman, there was no denying that, and Rick was under her spell.

"I'm here for a business convention. I'm in the brokerage game, top performer for the last five years. The vice president bowed out at the last minute and I have to fill his spot. I had expected to be bored to tears, but it's beginning to look as if I might actually find something to enjoy out of the trip." He slid the shot glass toward the inner edge of the bar and tapped it twice. "I'll have another, please, and give the lady whatever she likes."

"Thank you. Why don't we move to a booth? My legs get rather uncomfortable sitting this way for long." She stood slowly and stretched like a cat waking from a nap. The dress rode up her hips, offering another brief glimpse of her black lace panties. Deep red hair peeked enticingly through the lace, proving the drapes matched the carpet. Without waiting for a response, she sauntered to the last booth along the wall.

Geoffrey threw a ten on the bar and snatched both drinks. Slopping tomato juice over one hand and whiskey over the other, he wasted no time in joining her.

"Damn!" muttered Rick. There was no way now for him to hear their conversation. It wasn't that he wanted to hear her seduced by this Wall Street wonder. He just wanted to let her voice pour over him, hot and sticky. Listening to her for a while left him feeling like his whole body was covered in thick warm honey. Just once he wished she'd find no one to leave with, and then maybe he could have a chance. Deep inside he knew it was a fool's hope, but it was the only thing that got him moving each day.

The door opened again as a couple of regulars strolled in. A swirl of snow slipped in around them, stark white against the coal-black floor. They shuffled to the far end of the bar and pulled out a couple of stools.

"Damn!" Now he couldn't even console himself with watching her from across the room. He moved down the bar and set two mugs of beer in front of the old men. There was no need to ask; these two had nowhere else to go and would stay until he shooed them out. With a sigh, he turned on the television before they had the chance to ask. ESPN. He knew four beers from now they'd be deep in a heated argument about whatever the commentators had to say.

He stole a quick glance toward Donna and saw with frustration she was holding Geoffrey's hand between her slim white palms. He wondered what she was saying and bit back a dark, black ball of envy. He started a tab for the regulars, and smiled as a sudden inspiration struck. He quickly filled several small bowls with peanuts and moved about the room setting them out on every table. He tried to look casual as he eavesdropped on Donna and the stranger.

"So, what's such a beautiful woman like you doing here all alone on such a bitter night?" Geoffrey asked. He tugged at the knot in his tie as if it were choking him.

Rick shook his head and chuckled to himself. He was certain Donna would never fall for such a banal line. Not his perfect Donna. She was far too sharp. He was always there for her, and he took comfort knowing she trusted him. She had only to ask, and her words became his commands. Time and again she broke his heart, but Rick remained her willing slave.

"Oh come now, Geoffrey. I think you know exactly why I'm here. I'm here to meet you." Donna smiled across the table. Her teeth were perfect white pearls encircled by deep-red lips that matched her nails. "Let me know when you figure it out, and we can head back to your hotel room."

Rick watched as Geoffrey wiped a silk handkerchief across his forehead. The businessman cleared his throat and lifted Donna's hand to his lips, kissing it before speaking. His words came a bit too fast, and his voice cracked. "Oh, darling, I would love to take you back to my room, but shouldn't we discuss the arrangements first?"

"That will not be necessary," she whispered. "You just tell me what you'd like, and when we've finished you can tell me what you feel it was worth." She stood up and inclined her head his way.

Geoffrey leapt to his feet and reached for her arm. His stomach paunch caught the edge of the table, raising it a few inches before it fell back to the floor. Both drinks toppled, pooling in the center of the Formica surface, a mix of whiskey and tomato juice reminiscent of the effluvia his ulcer-ridden stomach often ejected.

Rick went to the back room, returning with a large towel over one arm and a full-length silver fox coat over the other. He held the coat open and Donna slid into it, her movements all liquid grace. She stood on tiptoe and kissed the barman's cheek.

Geoffrey glared and pulled a twenty-dollar bill from his money clip. He extended it toward Rick as if it were contaminated and he couldn't wait to be rid of it. He circled his arm around her waist and guided Donna to the door. Rick slammed his fist on the bar as he watched them cross the street and enter the Sheraton through the revolving door. He knew what was about to happen. It was not the first time, nor would it be the last though there was nothing he could do to change the situation. Donna was in complete control.

* * *

Geoffrey felt a fire burst into life in his loins, flames crackling from his testicles and up his shaft. He'd traveled a lot on business, and he'd seen more than his share of hookers in the hotel bars. He'd used a few, the kind who would give you a handjob for ten bucks. Anything more than that was risky business. He could just imagine the drama if he brought some parasite or infection home to the old lady. Hookers were not worth what the wife would put him through.

But this woman was beyond unbelievable! No one could ever call her a hooker, nor even a prostitute. Such appellations were far too vulgar to lay on her. Call girl wasn't quite right either. Maybe *Gentleman's Escort* would do he supposed, though he'd never seen an escort before. He hoped he had enough in his wallet for this.

As the elevator doors slid shut Donna rubbed her body against him, grinding her hips against his leg. He moaned. "Hold on, gorgeous, or I'm afraid I'll have to take you right here. I hate to admit it, but it has been a while for me and I don't know how long I can hold out."

Donna drew back and chuckled. "The best things in life are worth waiting for, you know. We have all night; there is no need to rush. Which floor is it?"

Geoffrey scratched his head, trying to retrieve the information. "Six! I'm on the sixth floor, room thirteen." He grinned, pleased with himself as if he'd just discovered the meaning of life.

Donna laughed out loud and pushed the button. She hummed a classical tune as the elevator rose, the lights moving up numerically until the door slid open on six.

She strode down the hall, moving like a jungle panther. She stopped and leaned against the wall, waiting in front of his room. Geoffrey pulled out the key card, dropped it three times and hit his head on the door handle. Donna took a quick, deep breath as a trickle of blood seeped down his forehead. She bent down, took the card and opened the door.

Donna laid her bag on the nightstand, turned on the lamp, took off her fur and then patted the edge of the mattress. "Why don't you sit down, get comfortable and tell me just what you'd like from me." As he sat, she leaned over him, her cleavage at eye level, and pulled off his jacket. It fell to the floor with a soft clunk.

Geoffrey thought for only the flicker of a moment, and then knew what to say. His wife would never give him oral sex, never had, not even once. Missionary sex was her only allowance, and the routine was choreographed with military precision. On and off, no more than five minutes, always the same. He'd endured the lifelessness of his marital bed for eighteen long years. The way he saw it he was overdue; he was long overdue.

"I want you to suck me. Suck me dry," he moaned. "Please take it, take it all, every last drop." He gasped as she nodded and unfastened his belt. He lifted his hips slightly to allow her to pull his pants and silk boxer shorts down to his ankles. His penis sprang up and stood like a flagpole capped by a purple dome.

Donna shimmied down to her knees as if sliding down an

invisible pole and took his throbbing organ in her delicate hands. Rapid bolts of electricity shot along its length, and the hair on his balls actually stood on end. Slowly she caressed him, rubbing the head up and down in her cleavage before opening her perfect little mouth.

Geoffrey's head fell back as he gave himself over to the experience. He'd read about this, seen it done in porno movies, but never had he imagined the ecstasy it provided. At first he closed his eyes, then realized watching his penis between her lips intensified his pleasure. He wished he could reach his cell phone in his suit coat's inner pocket. This was an image he wanted to capture for eternity, to be able to access again after his wife was snoring. He thought if he died tonight, he could die happy.

Donna's tongue teased the tip, then licked circles around the lip. Her mouth was cold, like a drink of water in July. He groaned as her hand moved up and down, squeezing and relaxing the pressure in a waltz-like rhythm. She slowly traced the thick pulsing vein on the underside of his cock, upward with her thumbnail and back down with her tongue. Her mouth opened wide and she took his entire length into her throat, all the while lapping with her tongue. She gave him her complete and unbelievable attention for what seemed to Geoffrey an eternity.

Suddenly he felt his testicles tighten, pulling upward. His cock grew harder than it had ever been and began to tremble. She slowed, pulling her lips up until they just barely held him. He leaned up and grabbed her, both hands pushing down on her shoulders.

"Oh, Donna, suck me! Suck me dry! Every last drop, please. Don't stop, please don't stop. No, don't you dare stop. Don't stop until you swallow it all," he moaned. His fingers dug deep into her pale skin, dimpling the tender flesh.

Donna lowered her mouth, letting his penis fill her throat. She flicked her left thumb and pressed the shooting star on her ring. Her mouth increased the suction on his member as the golden dome of the ring opened. From the small slit a fine golden blade like a miniature scalpel popped out. Just as his cum shot the back of her throat she sliced the blade through the thick throbbing vein, just beneath the head of his penis.

With ravenous joy she drank, as blood and semen mingled in her mouth. She purred with satisfaction as the fluids pumped from his softening organ. Geoffrey collapsed backward on the bed, his limbs feebly jerking. Still she continued to suck, now moaning herself as a smile of rapture lit her face.

When at last his body went still, she rose to her feet and smoothed her dress. She took her phone from her bag and sent Rick a text, telling him there was a clean-up required in room 613. She pulled on her coat, ran her long white fingers through her hair and felt a trace of wetness on her chin. She wiped away a single trickle, licked her finger and chuckled. "The customer is always right. I have to finish every last drop."

IT GROWS ON YOU
Ramon Mendes Jr.

1

Wilson had never seen anyone more beautiful. She was pictur-esque and he knew from the moment he had seen her that he was in love. She came into Bennigans one night, carrying with her a leather portfolio pad and the finest breasts this part of Clara City had ever seen. They were not the plastic-fantastic kinds that seemed fake the moment a set of sober eyes had glanced them, but indeed they drew harsh criticism from woman who's breasts had sank down to their kneecaps. They were succulent, and if caught on a chilled autumn day, her nipples sprang from her top like poignant beads. They were always on display and Wilson Hamling couldn't complain one bit, and if he could complain, it was more towards the fact that he couldn't blatantly masturbate when she waltzed into the tavern, lord knows, he had wanted to plenty of times.

Wilson, the bartender at Bennigans was a hopeless roman-tic. He fell hard for woman, and more often then not, they never truly fell hard for him. His blue eyes, a crystalline aqua, did nothing to help his sex life, but boosted the compliments. And what were compliments at the end of the day? A tease? Spoken words from a fine piece of ass that he surely was never to get? Why yes they were. Compliments came as he did, late at night in his apartment down in Eastern Edalys. He mastur-bated several times a day and to the good stuff. Thick ebony's, big breasted Latinas and the sloppy blow jobs only a skilled handler of the 'One Eyed Willie' could administer.

Leroy was the manager at Bennigans. He wasn't a bad looking fellow. His hair was always neatly slicked back expos-ing the jut of his widow's peak, his lips were as slick as his hair (he had this weird impulse to lick them every several seconds) and his build was solid. Broad shoulders, thick forearms. Wilson had even seen him turn the top clear off a bottle of beer with nothing but his arms clenched together. Of course Leroy walked with a massive limp. He was involved in a car accident five years prior. His right leg was mangled. Deep scars ran across his thigh all the way to his ankles. He covered them with tribal tattoos. He thought it hid the grotesquery of his wounds, Wilson disagreed. It was more than an injury; he was practically dragging his left leg along as if it had died from infection half a decade before. He stayed mostly behind the counter. He was insecure about it and Wilson couldn't blame him. It was a real sight. From behind the bar he would race (limping of course) to a seat at one of the rounded tables.

The dim lights of the tavern played into his favor. He could maneuver slowly amongst the shadows undetected, his gimp leg trailing unnoticed and free from unsettlingly stares. Despite the leg, Leroy got the ladies. He had mastered the art form of deceit and it was Wilson who played fetch.

"Round of Tequilas, Will! Make it snappy, come on. I don't want these beautiful ladies waiting." Wilson would pour it up with not a word of protest. He hated the treatment but mouthing off and losing a job that paid quite well was out of the question. He needed the job more then he needed pussy and even he was smart enough to realize that, for if that wasn't the case he would have told Leroy to come and get the rounds of Tequila himself if he needed them that bad. And what would Leroy have done? Gotten up? Dragged that poor excuse of a leg across the wooded floor before a table of woman? Wilson doubted that, but that didn't keep him from wondering.

Wilson always wondered about that, and what Leroy would have done in that situation. He pondered it, not incase he would indeed say such a thing, but to pass the time of his shift. The tavern was filled with woman at times, though none remotely interested in him. He was to serve liquor, garner tips and that was all. At times he even listened in (he did this on slow nights) to sensual conversations beside the table, cocking his ears forward, wiping down the bars table tops, even though it was as clean as a whistle.

He had been working at Bennigans for a full year when he first saw her. He didn't know her name, nor had he ever seen her before. She was new. She came through the tavern door looking this way and that, glancing over the sports memorabilia that hung on the far right of the room and the wall of photos from Bennigans yearly Beer Fest, dating all the way back since 1927.

She was rather amused by the décor, and from her grin, Wilson assumed she had considered it dated. She was in a tight skirt. It was a dark navy, and her top was a buttoned up business shirt, white and firmly pressed against her chest. There was a pen poking out of her breast pocket and Wilson wondered if he would be so lucky to be that ball point. He was that desperate. Her heals clicked as they strummed across the wooden floor, and when she braced the bar, leaning over in an amusing childish delight, Wilson knew he was in love.

"What you got?" she asked, and flashed a grin bearing a set of teeth that assured him she was meticulous and well groomed, aware of her looks and firm on the maintenance of her flawless beauty. She was perfect. From her neck dangled a feathered pendant, sterling silver perhaps, and when she pressed forwards it dully clanked across the bar top. He looked at, then beyond it. At her breasts. They were nestled in what seemed like a white laced bra and held firm in place.

"Hello?" she said again, rasping her knuckles across the wood.

Wilson recoiled embarrassingly and fetched for a row of the most common drinks banging several in a clumsy sprawl.

"Drink … drinks, oh yes. We have drinks."

She laughed, cupping her hands across her lips. "I know you have drinks," she said flatly. "But what kinds?"

"All kinds," he said.

She gave this some thought and sat atop a stool sighing as she did it and plopping a leather bound portfolio pad before her.

"Long day?" Wilson asked, aware now his words were coming smoothly. Stuttering chaps were signs of fear and uncertainty, and as long as he wasn't stuttering he considered that ok.

"You can say that," she said, passing a manicured hand across the table.

"Happens to the best of us," he said. "I haven't had a good day since I was 17," he confessed. *No!* he thought to himself, *Shut up. She doesn't want to hear that. Act normal for crying out loud!*

"Poor thing." She gave him a sympathetic pout of her lips, furling them downwards like a child having been told Santa wasn't real after all. She was so utterly adorable. Small dimples cratered her plump cheeks as she smiled at him. Her eyes so big and brown, he seemed to almost melt in her gaze.

"Well, I hope I brightened your day up," she said, "at least for the moment."

"You sure have. Miss …?"

"Brennan. Rebecca Brennan," she said.

"Well Miss. Brennan," Wilson said, reaching across for her hand, "I'm Wilson and it's a pleasure." She tipped her head welcomingly, brushing her brunet bangs off to the side. "Now how about I brighten up your days as you've done to me? What do you say? Mojito or a Georgian Peach? They both are quite splendid drinks."

She gave this inquiry no thought, and at the sound of Mojito she nearly leaped out of the stool and into his arms. "Mojito, oh how I love those. It's been a while since I've had one."

He spun atop his slick heals and proceeded to the rack of drinks. He was smiling. It was an odd feeling being on this side of the social fence for once. It was an out of body experience, almost a cleansing, and with a woman as beautiful as she, he was surprised he hadn't froze all together. It felt good, and he was loose and unafraid. It was this type of confidence that reaped the benefits. The pussy benefits.

He unveiled a glass from behind his large hands waving it before her eyes like a magician would with a trick or a hand of cards. She was engaged in his antics and stared in awe as he maneuvered his way through the recipe with such precision and certainty that being blinded folded would have been no more an impediment. He shot her a few glances as he squeezed the fresh lime juice.

She was moving gently with the tunes playing above, snapping her fingers and giving the tavern one good cursory look. "You've been working here long?" she asked.

"I made a year last week," said Wilson.

"How great," she said, letting her eyes drop to his ghostly moving hands.

"How about you? You work around here?"

"You could say that. I just moved into town a month ago."

Wilson rimmed the glass with fresh mint leaves, never once looking away from her. She was surely a sight. "How you like it out here so far?"

"It's fine. I can't complain."

He reached for the bottle of white rum beside the rack, flipped it into the air (he would have never done this otherwise) and clasped it just mere inches before it would have hit the table top. She drew back jubilantly at the spectacle.

"You're good!" she exclaimed.

"Practice. I'd like to think of myself as a pro."

He gripped a fistful of crushed ice from a cooling bin below the bar and filled her glass. He added several more mint leaves and adding just a splash of flavored soda, just for carbonation.

The drink sizzled and Rebecca gave a shrill cry. "Ooooooh. Looks good."

He dipped in a straw and slid it across the table to her. "One Mojito on the house."

She gave him that smile again, and without fail he felt his knees begin to buckle. She even awoke his genitals with that simple gesture of kindness, for his erection, a well endowed eight inches of cock was pressing faintly against his trousers.

She took a sip, letting the mint sheath her lips. Took a longer sip. Then a gulp. Her eyes fluttered in orgasmic bliss. "You're the best. If you only knew how much I needed that."

If you only knew how much I needed you, he thought. "It's my job to please you," he blurted and immediately and wished he hadn't. *No, why would you say that! She's going to think you're a pervert. She'll never come back. You're a jackass. A real scum bag!* Yet she took the comment in her stride playing along.

She gave him a wink. *Say it!* he thought to himself. If she had only known the apocalyptic showdown in his own mind, she would have fled in terror. *Tell her! No! Tell her now or never! I can't ...*

"I mean no disrespected Rebecca, but ..."

"Call me Becca," she said, sipping the drink now in large mouthfuls.

"Well Becca. I'm just curious as to-," He leant in closer to her, close enough to where he could smell the vanilla scent off her body. It was a pleasant smell, sweet like being in a candy factory, like fresh baked sugar cookies left out to cool. "What is a woman like you doing ..."

"Wilson!" A voice came booming through the tavern like a flaring gunshot. It startled Wilson so that he jammed up against the bar counter, faintly pushing his erection in. Leroy came hobbling across the bar, maneuvering through customers and heavy cigar smoke. "We got an order outside. I'll cover the bar while you head out and take the inventory, oh and don't forget to ..." He trailed off as his eyes glanced across Rebecca.

"Oh my!" he shouted, "Becca! I forgot! I'm such an ass!"

He waddled across towards her, the rasp of his leg scraping across the wood like a loose peg. He enveloped her in his large embrace, pecking her across the cheeks with light kisses. "I swear I forgot. It's this fucking job. It throws me off."

"It's fine," she said honestly. "I've been here getting acquainted with Wilson over there. He sure is a swell guy."

"Well don't get too acquainted pal," he said jokingly to Wilson.

Becca laughed innocently. Wilson did not. There was something in Leroy's eyes that made certain it wasn't a joke but rather a warning. A silent warning, those hidden with a dash of humor and a big old smile.

"Wilson, this is the tattoo lady I was telling you about."

"Hey!" Becca said in a scolding manner, tapping him across the shoulder. "I don't appreciate you gossiping, Mister."

"It's not gossiping," said Leroy.

Wilson was thus taken aback, not too far but far enough that he had to cock his head sideways as he always did in heavy thought. He remembered the conversation vaguely about some woman with a sprawling tattoo of some kind. A lion? No, maybe it was an eagle. Was it a serpent? Yes! It was the serpent.

"This is the serpent lady?" Wilson said uneasily.

"Yup. In the flesh!" said Leroy. "Her tattoo is bad-fucking-ass!"

Leroy *had* told him a story how he had met some woman outside during one of the deliveries. It was late August and she was scantly dressed, a strapless shirt of some sort, and how there was an intricate tattoo design, greatly detailed and etched sensually across her body. Wilson had dismissed it, but conversed for the sake of conversation. Women with tattoos aroused him the leased, except of course women who smoke, but neither got his blood pumping, so it came as a shock that this beauty who had so suddenly strolled into his life, had been the infamous serpent lady.

"Um, excuse me, Wilson. My name's Rebecca, not serpent lady."

"I apologize," said Wilson.

"Show him," said Leroy.

She shied away, pushing him softly to a distance.

"No!"

"Why not? Come on, it's a great tattoo. It looks good. You should show it off."

"So is pussy Leroy, but you don't see me flaunting my cooch around like a throwing Frisbee."

Great, Wilson thought. *She has a sense of humor. Dirty, but a sense of humor none the less.*

They all began to laugh nudging each other when the pain in there bellies were too much to suppress.

"Come on. Please. Show him. It's great."

"Ok, ok," she sighed.

Wilson leant across the bar top, tiptoeing for a better view, gripping the table just enough that he wouldn't summersault across it in a thunderous crash. She un-tucked her buttoned top from her skirt and lifted it barely. You could see skin. The lavender colored waistline of her panties.

"I can't see a thing," said Wilson, though he truthfully could not.

She raised it a little higher upturning her palms at an angle for Wilson's eyes and his eyes alone. There was a black and gray tattoo patterned and pebbled with reptilian skin. It seemed like a real serpent was slithering around her waist. It curled around the jut of her hip and seemed to dip across behind the small of her back.

"Wow," Wilson whispered. It wasn't the placement of the tattoo that rendered him speechless but the vivid portrait itself. The realism was magnificent. "That's amazing," Wilson said again.

"Told you!" Leroy shouted.

"Thanks, it's a work in progress," Becca said tucking her shirt back in.

"It isn't finished?" Wilson enquired.

"No. I had it started three years ago but stopped. I didn't like it, but after a while, I guess it grows on you like everything else."

Leroy leant in giving Rebecca a side hug and a gentle nuzzle with his nose. "So are we set for tonight? I got the car outside; we could go, just say the word."

"I guess. You still want to eat?"

"Fuck yeah," Leroy said clutching his stomach.

"I guess we can." She hopped off the stool grabbing her portfolio beside her. "It was nice to meet you Wilson," she said extending a small hand.

"Same here," said Wilson.

Leroy accosted Rebecca to the front door, arms around her delicate shoulders. Her ass was large and very fine. There was no sag in them, just a healthy jiggle. Wilson gave his cock a swift stroke.

"So you got it right?" Leroy said turning around.

"What you mean?" said Wilson, fixing up several drinks for the regulars.

"My appointment Wilson! Did you forget? I got an appointment with ..."

"Oh yeah, yeah. You got an appointment with Dr. Harper and you're on call for the surgery. I got the tavern Leroy, don't worry."

"Good man," said Leroy and almost sprinted out of the tavern with Rebecca despite that gimp leg of his.

"She's so great she can make a handicap run across like an Olympic track star," Wilson whispered to himself. The rest of the night crept slowly to its conclusion. He was tortured there all alone listening to old fucks whisper about the Derby races and blow stale smoke at his face. His mind was elsewhere, perhaps on if Leroy was actually fucking the shit out of that beautiful brunette, or how tight her twat must have been. How moist. He went home that night as eager as a child in a toy store. He masturbated three times before sleep came to him. He dreamt of her.

2

Each day at work was a day spent looking for her. He couldn't sit still for more then ten minutes at a time. It was so severe at points, that he would take leisurely strolls outside in hope, like Leroy, he would bump into her. For two weeks he heard nothing of her, neither did he hear anything from Leroy. He guessed he did get that call after all from Dr. Harper for the surgery on his leg. Harper practiced out of Boston, a thirteen hour drive from Clara, and Wilson assumed, given Leroy's leg, he was held up in some motel or patient recuperating center. He tried his home phone and there was no answer. Just the beep after the annoying moderator spoke her peace.

On the fifteenth day his worries were alas put aside. He wouldn't have to fear losing Becca for she was in front of him. He could hold her. Talk to her. He could speak and she would speak back. He had conversed with her plenty of times in his imagination. There, in his mind, he would play out these dirty scenarios.

She would be begging for it half the time (in Wilson's fantasies the women were always 'begging for it') and he would tend her needs. She would be asleep beside him and he would creep, as quite as a church mouse, as stealthily as a sly thief across the room to her side. She would be turned over, her hands neatly placed beneath her cheeks. So peaceful. So serene. His cock would be throbbing in his pajama pants, almost aching. Taking it out, feeling the warmth of it, the thick veins banded across the shaft like deep gashes. And with his cock out as hard as a steel pipe, he would rub it across her mouth. Up and down. He would go as far as his balls then back along the shaft, and at some point Becca would open her mouth, her eyes still shut and subconsciously begin to prod his dick with her wet tongue. She would soon wake, and upon realizing he was sliding his cock deep into her throat, she would not fight. She would accept it. After all she *was* begging for it, and so she would grip him in her hands and began to deep throat his cock until her esophagus began to swell.

It was a nightly treat, for Wilson dreamed this several times. Each time he awoke his trousers were drenched in cum, but on *this* day, the fifteenth day to be exact, Wilson was drenched in happiness. Becca strolled into Bennigans.

Their conversations were intriguing that night. They spoke about politics, conspiracy theory's and how downright sad she had been upon Michael Jackson's sudden passing. She came by every day for the next ten days. Leroy did not. He asked her about him. She had said that he had gotten the call after all and was safe somewhere recuperating from the surgery. It put Wilson at ease, at least for the moment. They sipped Mojitos, large glasses of Alize and several shots of Tequila. She paid for nothing. On the house meant she would soon be on him. It was a good deal.

When Wilson inquired about the tattoo again she showed him more. This time she was open and no longer shy. She lifted her shirt almost too high that the old geezers down the bar table almost fell out their seats. It was a snake-dragon combination sort of serpent. The skin seemed rough, but of course as he rubbed his hand along its side he felt nothing but her soft supple skin. The scales, thousands of them, diamond shaped, some oval, banded across her waist. He could not see its head, but could see that the tattoo indeed ran down the length of her inner thigh.

"It looks finished to me," Wilson said, "I wouldn't add a thing."

"It's not quite finished, here … look." She moved intimately closer to him turning around and giving him her back.

Then hitching her skirt down even more, she bent forward. The bar was basically empty at this time so there were no eyes they would need hiding from. Her panties were scarlet, thin laced with embroidered roses across the waistband, like a reef of fresh flowers. He moved back, just a little and dipped low on his knee. The serpent's body twined about her thigh like ivy to an old cottage. It looked vastly torsional and muscular and if he hadn't been as sober as he was, he was sure he would have mistaken it for a live creature. The tail of it wasn't at all complete. It simply vanished into her skin.

"I need to get the tail done," she said pulling up her skirt. "And the eyes."

"I haven't seen the head yet," Wilson said curiously.

She seemed to blush at this and brushed him playfully away. "The head is … well … It's private."

"I see," said Wilson giving her this devilish grin, flashing those big blue eyes of his. It only made his imagination churn with monstrous ferocity. Private? What did she mean?

They sat and talked the rest of the night. She spoke of her days back in New York and how the life, so fast and unforgiving, had exhausted her. She had needed an escape and Clara City had been just that. She spoke, he laughed, nodding in all the right places, but in truth he wasn't listening at all. The serpents head was running through his mind like a charging bull in the races in Pamplona. He wondered just where it was. His erection grew, died and grew again. The regulars came as usual, blowing their bitter smoke and fighting amongst each other for the horse biddings.

The day waned down, the sky turning a deep dark gray. That was more than enough to empty the bar. Most came afoot from their apartments. Rarely did anyone come by car. When the last regular (a guy named Peter Donaldson, a war veteran who always asked the hours of operation before he took his leave, despite that he had been a customer for over thirty years and the time of operation hadn't changed not even a minute) walked out, it was Becca who insisted he come home with her.

Wilson let Greta, the bars second tender, close up for the night. She had never closed on her own before, but knew, by the serious squared look in Wilson's eyes that it was important she do it. At least for tonight.

Becca and Wilson got into his Ford Contour just in time. The gray sky had finally broken. Rain gushed from above, swelling up the street gutters and potholes like small displaced lakes. As they drove, his heart was pounding. He literally thought it would burst in his chest and there he would die leant against the steering wheel, a hard dick in his trousers, promise on his mind and a fine beauty beside him he hadn't touched at all. He feared it would truly happen. He wasn't the most luckiest of men, after all.

There was silence in the car and so to ease the tension and awkwardness of the moment he put the radio on.

She snapped it off quickly. "I like the sound of rain," she said. "When I was little, I was frightened but I guess it grew on me."

"Like the tattoo," Wilson shot back overly excitedly.

"Yes," she said.

"It grows on you. It's life is it not?"

He couldn't help but realize she was staring at him the entire time he was driving. He tried to ignore it but his peripheral vision forced him to look ever so often and when he did, she would look away. He thought it was rather cute.

"I do like you," she said turning her body towards him. "I didn't think I would but ... here I am." She laughed mildly brushing her bangs behind her ear.

"I grew on you," Wilson said jokingly.

"I tend to have that affect on ..." and before he could finish she was running her hands along his thigh. He stuttered foolishly losing his train of thought.

"Go ahead," she said encouragingly. "You tend to have that affect on ..."

"Woman," he blurted, grasping for calm breath.

The wheel was slick in his hand. He was sweating and his balls were aching madly. He wanted to fuck the life out of this pretty little mama. Fuck her till she came. Fuck her till the night crept towards morning. Fuck her forever. He didn't know how he had made it all the way to her small apartment building with her teasingly touching him like that, but he did. He parked and cut the engine. Rain pecked against the steel roof like soft pebbles.

"Come in Wilson. Please. It's a rainy night; a girl like me could use someone to cuddle up with." She reached further along his thigh and closer to his crotch rubbing the tip of his dick with her palm.

She felt it, Wilson thought. He knew she had. He had felt her. He bit his lower lip and before he could reach for her, she was out of the car hoping over large puddles and a slick trimmed patch of grass. He reached into the glove box and tore open an unused box of condoms and was out of the car and into the lobby in a matter of seconds. She was already halfway into her doorway when he skidded into the lobby with his wet slicked sneakers.

She lived in apartment 1-A, the first of what Wilson assumed were twenty separate apartments in all. She waved a slim index finger gesturing sensually for him to come forward. He did, like a sheep to slaughter. When he entered he was pulled in violently and pushed up against the wall. The door was slammed behind him. She was nearly nude. Her skirt was off and her top hung together by three small buttons. Her panties hugged her frame amazingly. Her crotch was tight and he could see the faint outline of a camel toe impression.

Shoving her tongue down his mouth as she kissed, engorged his penis even more. Her lips were soft. She tasted sweet. He gripped her ass and lifted her. She moaned kissing him harder. Their tongues did battle as they latched to one another.

"Wilson," she moaned, "Wilson ... Oh ..."

He kissed her neck, sucking it faintly with his lips. *Like candy* he thought. Her breasts pressed against his chest. They were cool and delicate.

"Bedroom," she moaned kissing him again. "Left hallway ..."

He kissed her, digging his hands deep into her ass cheeks. They were soft as pillows, maybe even softer.

"Second door down," she directed, in a raspy whine.

With her latched across him he made his way to the bedroom. He lugged her across the bed where an arsenal of pillows flew across it and onto the floor.

"Oh my," she croaked unbuttoning the remainder of her shirt.

He sprawled on top of her knee bound, easing his hand beneath her bra. Her nipples were hard. He squeezed them tastefully as they again locked lips. She managed to shimmy his shirt off rubbing his chest, arms and neck.

"Fuck me Wilson," she called out. "Please, just fuck me."

In a breathless love lusted rage, he tore her shirt, clean off her body. The serpent was tattooed elegantly across the bridge bone of her breast and down along her left ribs, emerging then along the jut of her right hip. It turned him on even more. He pulled off her panties one handed as she propped her head comfortably on two pillows.

"Wilson, don't ... I ... I."

"Shhhh, baby its ok," he whispered.

He knelt closer to her pussy kissing it. She was shaved completely. There were no razor bumps he could see. No scarring...but... He looked a little closer and to his stunning amazement he knew alas where the serpents head had been. It was no longer a mystery. It was drawn purposely around the slit of her vagina, the slit itself being its mouth of course. It had no eyes. It was unfinished as she had said before, but still it seemed menacing.

She saw the troubled look in his eyes and tried to comfort him. "Told you it was private," she said thrusting her pubis into the air.

It truthfully didn't matter to Wilson. He was caught off guard that's all. She was wet and her lips gleamed in a glazed ooze, that made his mouth begin to water. He dipped low and pressed his lips firmly across the serpent's mouth. He licked her pussy running his tongue deep into the opening, licking her walls as would a child to a tasty lollipop.

This was grown man candy, he thought. *Sweets even a diabetic wouldn't turn down.* He couldn't believe he was chin deep in Rebecca's twat sucking and prodding his tongue along her clitoris. He dreamt of her. Wished she would be his. Wished he could have her if only for a brief moment and now, her she was, legs splayed and her body for the taking. She moaned louder gripping the bed sheets, arching her back. She was in elation and several moments from climax.

"Wait ...Wait," she breathed heavily. She pushed his head away and got on all fours. She gripped his belt buckle and he knew then what she wanted. It was stiff, hard and ready. She rummaged for his cock, pulled it out and without hesitation tucked it deep into her mouth. Her lips tightened as her tongue rubbed the tip, then, like in his many fantasies she ran it along the shaft. It felt great. Exhilarating! He stared off at the ceiling clenching his eyes shut. His vision was wavering. His father had always said he would go blind if he kept masturbating in his room all the time and now, seventeen years later, he would have to agree. He *was* going blind and loving every fucking minute of it.

Spit ran down her chin as she choked on his length.

"Argggggggchhh!" was the sound she made, pulling him deeper into her mouth. She wanted to choke it seemed. He gave a thrust deeper into her mouth until his cock briefly bent soothingly down the beginning of her throat.

She gagged and pulled him out. Bands of spit dangled like

silvery webs. "You bad boy," she said wiping the corners of her mouth.

He'd had enough. He wanted to fuck her. It was now or never. He couldn't wait. He nestled her waist and with brute force turned her around. Her pussy swelled from behind like a swollen fist. He ran his fingers threw it letting her juices douce the tips of his fingers.

"Go slow, Wilson ok? It's been a while."

He pushed her upper body down so her backside alone was up. Her back arched beautifully, and with the serpent tattoo slithering about her every curve, it made it that much better to look at.

"Ok," he whispered.

He let his cock dangle there for a moment considering the condom he had put beside the night stand. Fuck it he thought. He was too involved now and couldn't care less about the condom. He would fuck her raw and fuck her right. He came closer letting his dick rub the back side of her plump pussy. She whined when it touched.

"Oh go easy baby please. Go easy."

He gripped himself and slapped it along the serpents face, then as smooth as a knife to butter, he slid into her tender twat with a squish of suction. It was tight. It was more than tight. It was more like a vise. He loved it. He pushed in deeper.

"Easy ... Easy."

Don't get carried away, he thought to himself. *Go slow. Do it right and you might get a chance to do it again. First impressions go a long way Wilson, remember that. A very long way.* He fucked her slowly from behind listening as her wet cunt squirmed and spoke to him. Slowly he began to pick up pace and she didn't seem to mind. She took the cock like a champ and so he fucked her harder. Her ass plopped and danced like a fresh bowel of gelatin across his dick.

"Oh... Oh baby. Wilson... Oh. Wilson ... Wilso ..."

Their bodies clashed together sending sweat spraying

across his belly.

"Oh Rebecca!" Wilson shouted, feeling the pulsing throb in his dick as she grinded against him. "I'm coming baby! Oh god. Oh fuck! Fuck!"

She gave a hard thrust into him almost sending him backwards but he held his ground. He reached over and gripped her shoulders with both hands pulling her eagerly into him.

"Wilson! Oh ... oh. Wilson ... oh!" she cried out, now holding his wrist digging her nails deep into his flesh. "Fuck me. Fuck me."

He released her shoulders and gently ran his hands along her spine. His eyes barely open, he could see she was dripping with sweat. He wiped his forehead and braced her waist, but what he saw then far from amusing. It was downright terrifying. The serpent was moving! It slithered across her waist in slow turns. The scales were glazed with sweat. *No*, he thought, *that couldn't be. It was a tattoo, wasn't it?* He tried to ignore it. Surely it was the heat. He was simply hallucinating. Yes that was it. So much blood was gorging his penis that his brain was having withdrawals. He reached for the serpent. He had no fear. It was a tattoo and nothing more.

His forefingers rubbed the muscular amphibian. It recoiled at once. He sprang himself backwards hitting the door of Rebecca's closet on the far side of the room.

"What the fuck!" he shouted, gripping his chest. "What the fuck is that!" he said again.

Rebecca laid flat wiping sweat from her brow. Her hair was lightly pasted against her moistened cheeks and her grin, that grin he had been so fond of, that grin he had loved was no longer the same. Now it chilled him to his marrow.

"What happened Wilson?" she asked, drunkenly. "You don't want to fuck me anymore?"

"That fucking thing is alive!" he barked. "It's real goddamnit! It's real. I fucking seen it!"

"Oh poor Wilson," she said sourly, pouting her lip as she

did the first night he had met her. There was nothing cute about her. Not anymore. "It grew on me Wilson," she said coldly, "it grew on me and now it's a part of me."

She spread her legs wide holding them out so they made a large 'V' shape. The mouth of the serpent hissed and a black tongue ejected from its mouth and back in again. It crawled from her body as if it had never truly been attached at all. It hissed. Its eyes were black as beads.

"It's a part of me Wilson," she continued.

It plopped on the bed sheets like a thick black fire hose and began its trek across the bed, to the floor and finally towards him.

"Keep that fucking thing away from me!" he shouted at her.

He leant further onto the closet. He didn't dare make a run for the bedroom door. The serpent was large and he doubted he would make it. It would grasp him in an instant. It coiled itself forward letting its black parted tongue escape its mouth in sharp whips.

"Keep it back, you fucking bitch!" he scolded.

If he'd had known his night would have ended like this, he would have been more than happy to bust a load on a sheath of Kleenex tissues in his apartment. Anything but this.

When the serpent came but four feet before him, he opened the closet door and hid halfway behind it. Rebecca was erect on her knees watching as the snake proceeded menacingly.

"Poor Wilson," she said.

"It's ok. Don't be afraid. It grows on you. Before you know it, you'll like it as much as I do."

The hissing serpent made a lunge at Wilson, blasting its head through the closet's wooden door. Wilson at once felt a stiff pain. He closed the door holding the knob with his clenched hands.

"Stop!" he shouted, "Becca, please! Please! Stop!"

The serpents head retracted from the splintered hole it had made in the door and when it did, the dim light from the bedroom lamps flooded into the dark closet. It was then he realized his penis was gone. *Completely gone.* There was nothing but white tissue like bleached bone seeping out of a bloody stump. Blood was pouring out of him and the sight itself was enough to cause him to fall. His hands slipped from the knob and slowly, eerily, its hinges creaking in horrific audibility, began to open. Wilson was dizzy. He knew he was dying, it was just a matter of how. He reached for anything he could grab. Heels, a pair of sandals, empty shoe boxes, a leg. He didn't know it was a leg at first. He perceived it to be a bundled quilt of some sort, white and blotched with red pigments. But no. It *was* a human leg, and it didn't take him long to realize who it belonged to. Leroy's. It *was* Leroy's. The gimp one. The tribal tattoo along it had shriveled like a raisin. The skin was dead. Surely Leroy was as well. The leg he always dragged along Bennigans tavern, here it was, bloody and reeking of rot and decomposition. Rebecca only laughed at his finding. She said nothing. The serpent raised itself closer to Wilson's face, its tongue rasping across his forehead.

"It grows on you," she said.

Darkness came over Wilson. There was no pain. No nothing.

3

It wasn't long before Rebecca Brennan was back at it, strutting across Clara City in her finest business attire. Low trimmed skirt. Tight fitted top. It was at a stop light at 16th and Harbor that she met poor old Dennis Kinsley. He would be another piece to her ever growing serpent. He blessed her with compliments as the hundreds of poor souls who had came before him had done. It was her eyes that caught him. Yes, those sparkly eyes of hers. They were blue, a crystalline aqua's. They

IT GROWS ON YOU

were Wilson eyes of course but she wouldn't tell him that. No. Some things are better left unsaid as the old saying goes.

OVER TO OUR WEATHER GIRL FOR LIVE FEED

Nathan Robinson

It was by pure accident that I found her. I've been in love with her since I was about eleven or twelve with the prospect of an entire life ahead of me. I'm thirty one now, stuck with a shitty office job, cold calling folks who don't want to be called. Anyway, every weeknight at six twenty nine PM, she'd appear on our television. The brightest, most bubbly and sparkly weather girl I'd ever seen. She consumed me, every thought of lust I had was for her and I've been in love with her ever since. One way or another I wanted her, but I've never done anything about it, how could I?

She once opened a new science wing of a local college. I only found out about it in the paper the next day, but I got excited at the thought of her being in my town, close to me. The paper listed her as twenty-one year old, Kelly Weiss, with a picture of her cutting a ribbon with a pair of oversized scissors. Christ she was beautiful. Blond, tall and with curves in all the right places. What pre-pubescent boy, teenage male or fully-grown man, didn't find her attractive? My friends and I at school, would discuss how nice her breasts looked in that tight fitting red blouse she wore some days, or the fact that with winter coming up, maybe we'd be able to see her nipples proudly poking out to greet us through a particularly tight top.

Even when she moved to another television channel to present the morning weather, I dutifully obeyed and followed her. I found out that she covered the weather on the local radio station so I tuned my Walkman into her on the way to school so I could listen and fantasize to her dulcet tones.

Throughout the entirety of my secondary school life, she

was my fantasy woman. At night in my head, I convinced my-self that one day we'd be together as one, married with kids. I reckoned that she, having being ten years older than me, en-joyed the company of younger men, and by some miraculous stroke of luck on my sixteenth birthday (hopefully sooner) we'd meet and fall in love. She'd show me the ways of a woman and I'd satisfy her wanton needs that only I knew how, as no other man could manage. I imagined scenes where I rescued her from several life threatening situations where she'd always rewarded me with a lingering, passionate kiss. If ever I saw something remotely dangerous, I'd tell myself, *I could have saved Kelly from that.*

Even after I came back from university, she was still on the same channel, doing live weather and the occasional outside broadcast of a scientific nature, still just as beautiful, By then, I'd been through college and university, had my own experi-ences of real life woman, none of whom earthly beauties could be held up and be compared to hers. All tall, all blond, I never had another type. I even turned girls down of a different hair color, as it was easier to fantasize with a blond beneath me.

After ten years of fantasizing, I was still infatuated with her. I've never had a steady girlfriend as I've sadly always held onto the boyish dream that I was saving myself for her. I never revealed the extent of fantasy life to any one, not friends, family or the numerous lovers I've had to take her place.

I'd finished work early today. They let us go because of some maintenance work that needed to be completed on the fire alarms in our office. So after lunch, all the worker ants filed out into the Friday sun, with joy and an early drink on their mind. I joined my fellow co-workers for a quick pint or three, and then started the drive home. I needed bread, eggs and milk, life's essentials mainly, so I stopped at a shop on the high street close to where I live and bought my groceries. It was as I was coming out with my wares that I saw *her* across the street. I had seen the news and weather this morning and she was wearing the same tight white blouse that showed off everything I liked to the right proportions. Her hips swung her into a pet shop. With a boom of my heart and an unexpected river of sweat cascading down my back, I followed. Before I had chance to stop myself, the bell to the shop door rung above me and I was inside.

What am I doing here? was my immediate thought. *What do I say?*

I couldn't speak, let alone move my feet without thinking too much about it. The pet shop had that odor of sawdust and dry fish food. The owner smiled at me with a welcome nod then headed to the back of the shop. There, bent over and gazing thoughtfully through the tanks was Kelly Weiss.

"Be with you a minute," the shopkeeper said without turning.

"No worries," I somehow managed to say. My voice sounded high like I'd been gulping helium. I felt like I was twelve again.

With one hand holding tightly to my bag of shopping, I used my free hand to browse the dog toys, occasionally peeking towards the back of the shop to catch a glimpse of the delectable Kelly Weiss's sumptuous rump.

She was pointing at one of the many glass tanks; the owner nodded then headed to the back of the shop then came back seconds later with a brown paper bag which he handed to her. Then she followed him back to the counter, paid for what she wanted then headed to the notice and For Sale board that hung beside the doorway. I wanted to say something to her, anything. Tell her how beautiful she was, how she ignites the light of my day amongst the bleak grayness that is my dismal office imprisoned life. I couldn't say anything like that. It would be weird.

"Can I help you, sir?" the pet shop owner asked. It took me a few seconds to gather an answer as I was gazing in awe at the delightful golden strands of Miss Kelly Weiss's hair.

"Err ... Yeah I'll have this please." I handed over a rubber chicken chew toy that I had absently picked up from the shelf. I don't even own a dog, or any pet for that matter. I took my time gathering my change, I knew that if I stalled, I could follow her out of the shop, make it look purely natural. I still hadn't got a good look at her face up close, but I knew it was definitely her. She took out a notepad and pen and jotted down a number from one of the for sale notices. I gathered my change from the purchase of one number rubber chicken chew toy, taking my time to quickly count it without seemingly like a weirdo, then dropped it into my pocket.

By then the entrance bell had rung and the elusive Miss Weiss had left the shop, brown paper bag in hand. I nodded good day to the pet shop owner, grabbed my rubber chicken and dumped it in my grocery bag, then left.

Miss Kelly Weiss headed right out of the shop doorway, so did I. Slowing down, I looked casually at my phone, my idling fingers toying and pretending to work some important function. Ahead, Kelly Weiss read what she had just written. Ever so often I glanced up from my phone and caught a sneaky glimpse of her butt, twice I almost bumped into a fellow shopper as I gazed lovingly at her behind. Somehow it still hadn't completely sunk it yet that it was her. What do I do next? Ask for a photo? An autograph? What?

She stopped.

So did I.

She shoved the notepad back into her handbag and then fished around for something. I kept back, moving my eyes from my phone to the back of her head quite rapidly. Any passers by would think something wrong with me. She removed her mobile phone and dialed a number and rummaged in her bag, whilst I heard a floppy plop on concrete. She started speaking to the person on the phone and clicked the key fob; the hatchback closest to her blinked its lights, then she climbed in, talking on the phone as she did. I could see her through the windscreen, chatting with wide, excited eyes, her glorious smile spread across her face. I turned my eyes down to my phone just in time for her to look at me, her eyes caught mine briefly. I burned red and my heart started hammering again, faster and louder than when I first saw her. Do I smile? No, I was simply in her field of vision that was all. She didn't even know I was there in all probability, just another face in the crowd to her. Besides what chance did I have of ever talking to her? I couldn't get my words straight at the best of times, how could I ever talk to the love of my life? Her eyes burned through me, piercing my soul and out of my back like a high velocity laser beam, straight through everything that was I, without so much as a care or second glance. She dropped the phone into her bag, started the engine, pulled out and drove away, and then she was gone.

On the pavement where she had just stood, lay her notebook. The open pages waved casually in the wind, waving me closer. I turned; her car had reached the end of the street and was now waiting at the traffic lights that quickly turned red, leaving her first in the queue to turn left in the filter lane.

I had an in.

I picked up the notepad and started jogging up the street towards her awaiting car. The lights turned green and she pulled away. I had no choice. Life or fate or whatever twisting manipulation of the universe, had smiled down on me today. I had an in. An in with the girl of my dreams.

My car was across the street. Dodging traffic, I wasted no time in jumping in the driver's seat, tossing the notepad on the passenger seat. I started the engine and gunned the engine after her, narrowly avoiding a collision with several other motorists that also occupied the roads on this busy Friday afternoon.

I reached the lights; they stayed green for me as I screeched around the corner after her hatchback, seeing three cars ahead of me.

Don't chase her, you'll scare her off. Play it cool. *Hey you dropped your notepad, I saw you drive off. I thought you might need it. I hope you don't mind me following you. Say, do you fancy going for a drink sometime?* I mused in my excitable mind. Corny as hell. She'll probably scream and run away or call the police. Maybe she'll be grateful.

Or maybe she'll call the cops.

No, she didn't know me. She didn't know that I harbored a secret lust for her for over half my life. Just two perfect strangers. That was all. One human being helping out another. It's natural; it's what good people did for their fellow soul.

Oh, you're a weather girl? Well you've certainly got the looks for I …

Her car disappeared round a corner, the lights ahead of me turned red, the car in front stopped so I was forced to slam on the brakes to avoid a collision. The tires squealed a little in protest, clearly reflecting my frustrations at the time. I glanced down at the notepad whilst I eagerly waited for the lights to change. Her dainty writing spelt out an address, the numbers and letters of which immediately correlated in my brain to an actual location.

57, *Lower Smith Street.*

I knew that street. Hell, it was near the edge of town, barely five minutes drive, in fact it was the way she was heading. It was worth a shot.

I smiled while waiting for those last precious seconds before the lights turned green. Gunning the engine round the corner, I followed her trail with a hope in my heart.

It took me less than five minutes to get to Lower Smith Street, but as I got there, she was leaving number 57, waving goodbye to the owner whilst carrying a cardboard box under her arm. I looked for a place to park, but the street was chock-a-block with vehicles. She reached her car, put the box on the passenger seat then went around and climbed into the driver's seat. My heart started to beat hard in my chest, evaporating the air from my lungs. I felt faint and excited at the same time as the fluster overtook me like a virus. With the notepad in hand, I started to get out so I could call to her, but an irate driver behind me started piping their horn at me to move me on. I cursed and got back in by which time Kelly had started her engine and pulled out. The driver behind me waved me forward with a demanding flick of his hand. Seething at the missed opportunity, I carried on following the beautiful Miss Weiss's car.

I reached the main street at the end of the road and turned left, as Kelly had done. The hazy sun had started its melt into the afternoon; pedestrians ambled about while cars clogged up the streets. It soon became a struggle to keep up with her as she left the confines of the city, but the traffic cleared the closer we got to the outskirts. Soon it was just her and me following behind on the little roads. I kept my distance as to not alert her, sometimes dropping back by reducing my speed then catching up with her on the next corner.

Half an hour out of the city, we reached her home where she pulled into the driveway of a semi-detached little cottage on the outskirts of a quaint little village. Flowerbeds filled the south facing front yard with multi-colored delight, a line of confiners split the gardens on the two adjoining properties. The neighbors had a FOR SALE board stabbed into the border of their overgrown, yellowing lawn.

It looked like we were alone. I carried on up the road for about a mile then turned into a field of gently swaying corn, and for whatever reason, I waited.

Now this would look weird. Me, just turning up on her doorstep. I should have just pulled straight into the driveway and handed the notebook over. I couldn't exactly say I followed her home, and now I've left it a while, it would be even stranger turning up on her doorstep. She'd ask how did I ever find her, then probably call the cops on me. I've truly fucked this up. I should have left it, or tried harder to get the notepad to her.

I could just post it through her letterbox.

But then I'd never get a chance to meet her, never begin that fantastical romance I've always dreamed of and lusted after.

Screw it. Fuck it. I'd be honest with her, just tell her the truth, reveal that I recognized her from the breakfast news and that I saw that she'd dropped her notepad and I followed her home to reunite her with it. That was all. Nothing creepy about that. I wouldn't mention that I was deliriously in love with her. I'd hold that little nugget of information back for now.

I looked down at the notepad and picked it up. Just a traditional reporter's notepad, filled with notes. I started flicking back through the pages. Addresses took up the majority of writing, occasionally they'd be a little side note that led into the mundane routine of her life such as *PAY ELECTRIC BILL,* or *BOOK DOCTORS APPT.*

But the rest was just addresses that were nothing to do with work or meteorological musings. Pretty soon a pattern emerged from each of the addresses. I expected the addresses to be that of places of interest for when she did outside broadcasts, such as the long last week she did on coastal erosion of the east coast, or that new fossil that was discovered on a local archaeological dig. I expected addresses of museums and professors of such and such sciences.

But no. The pattern became apparent by page three of her notepad.

Four Winds Dog's Home.

Little Lucky Cat Rescue.

Belvedere Animal Sanctuary.

Page after page of animal rescue centers, at least eighty pages worth of addresses.

She must really love animals.

I dropped the notepad back on the seat, thought fuck it, then pushed my car back into gear then headed back towards Kelly Weiss's house.

I pulled up outside her neighbor's house, got out with the notepad in hand and headed for her front door. I mentally crossed my fingers that this went well; praying to whatever deity was listening that I would get what I always secretly wanted. *To get inside Kelly Weiss.*

I knocked on the door. Lightly, not too loud.

Hi, you dropped your notepad outside the pet shop. I hope you don't mind, but I followed you home. Would you like to go on a date sometime? Yeah sure, that's how it'll go.

I knocked again.

No answer.

Maybe she'd taken one of her many pets for a walk? She had vast fields to the back of the house so that might not be entirely unlikely.

I knocked once more then headed round the back of the house where I found the rear garden to be as pristine as the front.

A splash of water near my feet made me look down. I smelt soap. Water cascaded out of the white pipe and into a drain. She was having a shower up stairs, that's why she didn't answer the door. I looked through the kitchen window and spotted the box she had collected from Smith Street on the breakfast bar along side the brown paper bag from the pet shop. I headed further round the back, just to have a nosy round her garden, passing a corrugated roofed, pebble dashed garage. I crossed over a red and yellow chessboard slabbed patio area and onto the grass. At the bottom of the garden a shed had been converted into a chicken hutch, several hens pecked around the dusty soil within the meshed in area.

She obviously spent a lot of time out here crafting nature to reflect her beauty. Each tree was ornately sculptured, flowerbeds containing a multitude of vibrant colors lined down either side of the long garden. A raised bed constructed from old railway sleepers contained an abundance of vegetables whilst the greenhouse, which she had clearly been thinking greenly, was constructed out of plastic bottles speared on bamboo canes, containing tomatoes and peppers bursting with juicy summer flavors. Christ she was some kind of ecological genius. I marveled at her ingenuity.

Music erupted from within the house so I headed back up the garden to investigate. Reaching the back window I peered through. I looked over the shoulder of the beautiful Miss Kelly Weiss as she sat at the breakfast bar. A radio out of sight had been turned on, pouring a harmonious hum of classical music. My excited knuckles were seconds away from knocking on the glass when I watched Kelly Weiss open the brown paper bag. She took out a plastic tub about the size of a takeaway carton, then removed the lid, reached in with her fingers, then re-placed the lid as if to stop whatever was inside escaping. Then casual as ever she popped what looked like a small brown twig into her mouth.

My first thought was bemusement. Who buys Twiglets from a pet shop? Then as she reached in again and popped another one into her mouth, I saw a multitude of thin legs fighting her off before she crunched it between her ever-white teeth.

Crickets.

She was eating Crickets.

Straight into her mouth.

Raw and alive.

She didn't cook them or anything, they were still moving as she popped then into her mouth, squirming and fighting against her crunching, grinding teeth.

She fed herself another.

Raw and alive.

I watched transfixed, mesmerized by this spectacle that unfolded before me. Was she really eating them alive?

84

OVER TO OUT WEATHER GIRL FOR A LIVE FEED

In the space of five of the strangest minutes of my life she finished the entire tub, finishing the strange starter with a sexual shudder that even made me shiver in spite of the warm summer air that enveloped me.

It must be some mind of new fangled African diet, where you have to eat only citrus fruit, raw vegetables and insects. Celebrities were always promoting new fads in eating; this was just the latest craze. Hell, probably right now Beyonce was eating a bowl of mealworms and muesli in order to help trim down the baby weight, Brad Pitt was tucking into starfish burgers to bulk up for next role as Lion-O in the new Thundercats movie.

Latest crazes, that was all.

I watched as she worked a toothpick in between her teeth to dislodge any of the cricket's remaining limbs. She licked her lips when she was done, then reached into the cardboard box from Smith Street.

Oh no.

Furry, cute, fluffy.

This shouldn't be happening.

Reality defied the situation.

She had a black and white kitten in her hands. She held it aloft as if inspecting it for quality, turning it in the light as it meowed at being disturbed from the cosines of its box.

I shouldn't be here, my panicking brain told me. I was dreaming a living nightmare. Get back to the car and go. Any attraction to the still beautiful Kelly Weiss had quickly faded into the ether of the approaching night. I couldn't look at her in the same way again without changing my sexual preferences to completely weird.

I backed up as she brought the kitten towards her mouth, even as I left I was still transfixed, I couldn't take my eyes off of her.

My foot backed into something hard, it shrieked a terrifying metallic scrape as I tripped back with an all too deafening clatter. The watering can shot from underneath my feet as I kicked out and crashed down on the hard, unforgiving patio slabs, landing hard on my elbows. My funny bones had nothing to laugh at, yet they screamed in painful delight.

I was in the process of getting to my feet when a florescent light over the patio area burst on brightly. A shadow rushed towards grabbing something then stood over me.

"Wait!" I pleaded before a whoosh and something heavy and shovel shaped clanged down across my skull. Then the lights went out.

I have the briefest sensation of being dragged over the warm patio slabs; the back of my head is wet and eases my transition, softening the scrape. A rusty garage door screams open in protest then I fall headlong into dreamless sleep, held hostage by dark, empty thoughts.

* * *

A belch tore through the silence of my dead end dreams.

"I started on worms when I was little, my mother always told me not to, but I did." The voice was soft and melodic, soothingly familiar. I tried to crack open my eyelids; dim light illuminated my world.

"My parents sent me to a psychologist, an old guy who I discovered to my advantage that he liked little girls. I got him round my finger and he soon signed me off as being what you would call normal. Just a phase he told my mother. After that I carried on my hobby in secret. Apart from him and you, nobody knows my little secret that I've discovered."

I murmured a hazy reply. Not even I knew what I'd meant.

"The big fat Lobworm was my favorite when I was a little girl, so juicy and full of flavor. I spent a lot time in the woods as a teenager, armed with a shovel. I spent hours foraging until I had a good bucketful then I'd wash them all in a nearby stream to get any soil off and then pick them out one by one. Every time was a treat really. Better than chocolate."

I forced open my eyes. The overhead florescent burnt my corneas for a second before my eyes adjusted to the interior of the corrugated garage roof. In my daze I tried to sit up, instantly feeling the tight bonds that held me down. I swallowed a dry and chaffing lump that charred my throat. I felt hoarse. I remember screaming at some point during the blackout. I tried to part my lips to ask why. But it appeared that they too were victims of bondage.

I shifted my gaze left. Kelly Weiss stood nude, the gloom sparsely clothing her modesty. I could make out her toned stomach, seemingly full and pregnant sitting beneath firm breasts pointing at me with proud almost edible nipples. She looked wet and slick like a battle-ready warrior queen. Even after what I had seen her do, I still had urges of lust for her. I still hungered to climb on top of her and just take her, ravish her till her insides caught fire and we collapsed into each other's sweaty orgasmic abandon. She was still the woman for me; I couldn't imagine myself with any one else. So it had brought me here, to her house, taped up and naked in her garage.

Secretly and sickly I hoped she'd rape me in some way.

"Don't scream," she said softly, tearing the duct tape from my mouth. 'The closest neighbors are in the village, so they won't hear you. I needed a rest, maybe a talk, now where was I?" She cast her eyes aside as if thinking back, her memories lost somewhere. Then, "Ah yes, then I started on mice and rats. We couldn't get any real meat as the war had started, but still I manage to get my daily dose of protein."

"What?" I managed to croak, shivering because of the cold on my skin.

"The war. We didn't have much to eat. I always brought my mother back some mushrooms from the woods, she knew which ones to eat. She was clever like that."

"What war?"

"I think you know. Don't play dumb."

"I'm not."

"You're my first you know. I've never had any one else, human, I mean. The guilt would be atrocious. I just couldn't. I've always been curious though. I've never wanted a man, or woman for that matter. Sex never interested me so I never got intimate with anyone, no one ever got close enough to know my secret. It's been nice to finally talk about it. I've always thought about writing about it. Everything I've done, my secret. Let them find it when I've gone. But it'll be years before that happens." She smiled, this time casting her eyes down to the floor. Then she looked back at me.

"I don't think I understand," my voice was raspy, but seemed to be clearing.

"I never told anyone what I do in my spare time. I tell people that I read, or turn my telescope towards the stars, which I do. Sometimes. But my real passion is food." Her eyes seemed to light up with a phosphorus glow as she stepped closer. "I love to eat."

The haze that had clouded my eyes cleared and my vision focused. Dark stains had dribbled down her chin, the soft line of neck, cascading over and around her sumptuous breast, down her full belly and into the furry blonde V of her crotch.

Red stains.

Blood.

The pain rose in a suddenly stinging wave, my legs felt strange, a scream fought its way out of my throat. Kelly quickly slapped the duct tape back over my lips and held it there. I struggled to get up fighting against my bonds. I manage to raise my head enough to see the startling white bones of my legs, my meatless toes stared back stark white, held together by fatty looking strands of sinew tendons. All the skin and muscle had gone, she'd licked the blood off of my bones up to my kneecaps, above that on the bulging flesh of my thigh, she had tied tight twine to staunch the blood flow. It had worked a little, but still blood had coagulated in a darkened puddle on plastic sheet she had laid me on.

She caressed my forehead with delicate strokes of her warm fingers, whispering soothing sounds into my ear.

"Please just relax. I don't want you to die on me. It wouldn't be right. It alters the taste of things. I promise you'll be the last and the only one. You found my notebook didn't you? I can't let my secret get out. It would ruin me. I enjoy my life and I intend on doing so for a lot longer. I know I'm nice to look at, so I'd like to stay this way as long as I possibly can."

I tried to say, "I won't tell, I won't tell!" but it got garbled into nonsense against the stuck fast duct tape.

"Shush, shush my sweet. If you want, I can knock you out again. I usually do that with bigger feeds when they struggle. It makes the meal easier to digest. I always test for a pulse, and as soon as they die I stop eating, otherwise it doesn't work as well. Dead flesh does nothing but block you up. It's got to be a live feed. It's the only way it works."

Terror paralyzed me, but an overbearing lust for this woman overtook, encouraging my mindset to just accept what was happening to me. This was meant to be. This was my destiny with this woman. Somehow, in this twisted world of ours I accepted it.

"I'll leave your car by the river up the road with your clothes inside. It'll look like a suicide. I'm smart like that."

I offered a vague smile at her ingenuity. My co-workers would believe that. They all knew I hated my job. I would have never thought of it. I was to disappear from this world and it would be with the most perfect woman imaginable. If I were to go anyway, I'd be happy if it was this way. In fact I was.

"Anything left I'll cut up for the chickens, your bones will be ground up and spread on my perennials, so you won't go to waste. I like to recycle."

I started to laugh, heaving a great lungful in through my nose and then crying out in delirious, stunted guffaws, each muffled by the sticky duct tape on my mouth.

Kelly untied my right arm from the table that I was lashed to. She had already tied tight twine around my elbow.

"I'm hungry again. It doesn't take long once you get into the routine of eating big meals. I like to run a lot so I usually burn it off."

She smiled with perfectly straight blood soaked teeth then raised my hand to my mouth and bit into the fleshly part between my thumb and palm, bright, glorious blood ejaculated across her face and neck as she chewed and nibbled warm flesh away. I smiled sickly and watched in semi-insanity as she started to finish off the meal of consuming me. Finally I had her. One way or another I had her. I was going inside Kelly Weiss.

COOKIES
Paul Edmonds

All twelve of them had their dicks out for the whole world—or at least everyone in the apartment—to see. It was quite the eclectic mix. Long ones. Short ones. Thick ones. Thin ones. It was known around their neck of the woods as Kookie Cookie. There are, of course, regional variations on the name depending on where you choose to drop your drawers and pull your prick, but the basic rules are always the same.

The first thing you do is make sure that you and your crew ingest enough intoxicants—take your pick, doesn't matter really—so that the whole idea sounds like something worth doing.

Second, you select your cookie. For some reason the cream-filled sandwich variety is very popular on the spunk-dumping circuit, and that's what was on the floor that night.

Third, you form a circle around the cookie. The ideal circle consists of no more than six participants. Any more than six and the diameter of the circle becomes too large and some of the guys have trouble with the distance. We're looking at twelve here, so picture a good two feet between each guy and the innocent confection.

Fourth, each athlete pulls his pants and underpants down to his ankles.

And lastly, all the guys start beating off. The guy at the end who hasn't sprayed on the cookie has to eat it.

The crowd was rowdy. The raucous cheering grew louder, threatening to reach a crescendo that would blow out the windows. A symphony of slaps and grunts completed the soundtrack, with a few "fuck yeahs" and "oh gods" sprinkled in for an added layer of ambiance.

Expressions of every fashion adorned the faces of the

onlookers: bemused; sickened; appalled; amorous. One girl turned around and left, a red fist clenched around car keys. A lady friend of one of the chaps, no doubt. The swarm moved closer to the contestants, breathing hard and swilling beer between chants. The humidity was stifling and condensation began to form where the walls met the ceiling, like the many droplets of sweat crawling down the arms and faces of the brave men determined to charm their snakes.

One of the tuggers, a lanky boy with a wan complexion and scratches on his arms, groaned the grunt of some brooding beast and bit down on his lip until a stream of blood rolled off his chin and disappeared into his coarse pubic hair. A moment later ropes of semen fired from his penis and landed on the cookie with incredible accuracy. The fans went wild. A girl of unfortunate appearance danced around while pretending to ride an invisible bull.

The second guy came. Then the third. Then the fourth and fifth in concert. Each new eruption triggered uproarious laughter and applause.

Carol watched all of this from her spot across the room. A break in the crowd afforded her an unobstructed view of the action. The game had been her idea. It was her turn to make collections, as she and her girls had come to call it. Invariably, parties were the way to go. There were always a lot of guys to choose from, and a quick round of frost the cookie would gather more than enough sweet plums in one fell swoop. All she had to do was toss out the idea, and some drunkard would run with the ball.

The tired tragedy played on. Carol could usually call the winner, but she failed on this particular evening; her guy drained his balls shortly after some portly loser who was forty years old if he was a day. The remaining two guys toiled about for a good ten minutes in a fit of cramped hands and peeled skin. Carol passed the time by naming them Number One and Number Two. She smiled, and already a stirring in her pants raised her nipples against the thin purple polo shirt that clung to her svelte body. Tiny hairs perked on the delicate flesh of her ears. It was getting late. They were awaiting her return.

Finally, Number Two popped off, and the contest was over. Number One looked half-dead. He pulled up his britches and knelt in front of the cookie. Talk about a mess. A hush stole over the panting crowd. Number One looked from face to face, desperate, hoping for an acquittal, but one was not issued. He poked at the cookie with his index finger. He picked it up gingerly and brought it to his mouth with the delicate movement of an old lady with a tiny cucumber sandwich.

After a good fit of the dry heaves, Number One started for home. He brushed along hedges and parking meters as he swayed from left to right in a seemingly endless impression of a ship on choppy seas. Carol followed close behind, moving in and out of shadows. Her left nipple pierced the fabric of her shirt. It had turned to metal and caught the moonlight brilliantly.

Number One stopped in the middle of a deserted intersection, patted his pockets, and came up with a half-crushed pack of smokes. He pulled one from the box and pressed it between his dry lips. He searched for his lighter. It was nowhere to be found.

Carol approached. Her siren-red lipstick burned orange under the dull yellow streetlight.

Number One stared at her with a queer look. "Hey, didn't I see you back there?" he said, his words more pureed than slurred.

"I bet you did." Her voice was sweet and lovely. "I believe we passed each other in the hall."

Had the light been better, Number One would have caught a fleeting glimpse of Carol's black forked tongue as it danced about to form her words.

"Are you following me?" he said, and rubbed the back of his neck.

"Of course. I took notice as you were leaving. I thought I'd see you home." Her right nipple broke through her shirt. A matching pair.

Number One saw this and bent down to get a closer look. His breath cast a fog over the sharp, shiny protrusions. "What? How did you do that?"

The seat of Carol's jeans grew hot and damp. Her tongue thrashed against the back of her teeth, then fell from her mouth. It licked wildly at the cool night air. Claws as thick as bamboo shoots grew from underneath her fingernails and bore deep red canals in the tips of her fingers. Number One glimpsed three seconds of high cheek bones and tiny hooked teeth before the streetlight was snuffed and everything fell silent.

Carol cradled him in her arms and retreated into the muted shadows of that sticky-hot summer night. She and her girls would work quickly to disassemble Number One's stomach before the rolling fizz of acids stomped out the viability of the swimmers inside of him, the crucial ingredient needed to propagate their dwindling populace. A human Petri dish full of life and possibilities, an entire world clinging to the masticated remains of a single fateful cookie.

MESMERISM AND CHLORO FORMOR BAD PENNY MAKES CHANGE

Douglas Payne

A dull couple approaching their autumn years were watching the evening news. The drooping stock market showed no sign of recovery, flopping like a wet fish before death. There is mention of the new health care bill that is floating around in Congress, waiting on a vote. The husband does not know what to make of it. He was laid off from work last month. His family has no health insurance.

His daughter Penny occupied one of the rooms upstairs. On her dresser was a stand-alone CD player, which rested atop some old equalizer that she had bought at a garage sale along with a pair of speakers. She also had a subwoofer there. A well enough sized hole was visible in the driver.

This dated audio setup had a futuristic appearance that bordered on the comical. The pressure of the volume, three quarters of the way up, was causing the illuminated control buttons to shake loose. The speakers were blaring some grating industrial music from the late eighties.

Penny had the door of her bedroom locked. She was sitting at the computer with headphones on, dressed in red flannel pajamas and a plain looking bra. A grainy video is on the screen. Penny takes off her glasses and wipes them on her pants to obtain a clearer view of the picture.

In the film, there is a girl in a car with two other men. They look Russian, but they could be Romanian or Czech or a host of other things. They seem in good spirits. The driver shoves his face towards the camera, his eyes shining. He aims it towards the man in the back seat. This one has a sly grin on his olive colored face, his arm slung about the girl's shoulder. She is blond, about twenty years old. She had that sameness about her so ably found in young women on any downtown street in an American city. She was laughing at something one of her male companions had said, something muffled and unintelligible to Penny through her headphones. The short fit of laughter from the girl's throat had been unnatural and deliberate. She squirms around on the beige leather interior, tugging at her seatbelt. Her eyes hold the emotion of a steel post.

A rough cut to the next scene.

The girl and the two men are in a motel room. There is a wet rag on the floor. A dim lamp lends an orange coloration, the surroundings casting shadows on the faces and limbs of the two men as they move about the room. The camera is mounted on a tripod now, at an adjacent angle to the corner of the bed. The girl sits on the bed, naked and dazed. Her arms and legs are browned, but the rest of her is white like ivory. Except for her face, which is flushed red. The man who had sat with her in the car, the one with the sly grin, kneels down and pushes open her legs. The expression on Alyssa's face, the slight movements of her body, tell that she is divided between reluctance and yielding. After some brief moments, she leans back on her hands and tilts her head up, closing her eyes.

The other man, the driver, walks into the shot and obstructs the camera's view. When he moves away, all that can be seen of Alyssa is her legs. The man's bald head still wedged between them, beads of sweat cascading down his crown. The visible presence of the young girl stops right before her breasts would begin to show. Her torso is twisted to the right and her side demonstrates a gradual slope upward. In quick flashes, the hand or arm of the driver can be seen creeping into the frame. He is standing by Alyssa's chest. Or her head. Small grunting noises can be heard.

Not another fucking dud, Penny thought.

The man outside of the frame walks into the view again,

blocking camera. He is hiking up his jeans. Then he is gone again. Exit stage left this time.

The other man comes up from between Alyssa's legs now and lays his body on top of hers. All that can be seen is a mess of legs. Erratic thrusting. The audible commotion from the fabric of his jeans brushing against the bed. Alyssa shouting, "stop." The rough gurgling sound of her choking. The man stands up. Hikes up his jeans. Clears his throat.

Alyssa is whimpering. Saying in a quiet voice, "Why?"

The man walks to the far side of the room and stands by the door.

The camera zooms out. A full view of the room is presented. The man still stands by the door. Alyssa's shaking body is crumpled up on the bed. The camera lingers on her for awhile, stationary save for the jagged moving of an unsteady hand. An excited hand. The crystalline tears roll down her face.

Penny's hand was inside of her pajamas, moving at a rapid pace.

The driver comes into the edge of the frame. Enter stage left.

Alyssa shoots up, her eyes wide with unbelieving. She screams and causes Penny's ears to ache with a sharp stabbing hurt. Penny knows what is coming. She is overcome with anticipation. Her mouth is dry and her heart is racing. Her hand is moving inside of her pajamas, faster and faster.

The driver lifts his arm to show the cold black steel of the gun. Alyssa screams again before an explosion rattles in Penny's brain, a loud burst of noise that blocks out the shrill sounds of her own voice created by her peaking ecstasy. Like the squeak of a mouse.

For a split second the camera allows the terrible vision of the bloody crater in Alyssa's chest before all goes dark. Nothing lingers and nothing can be comprehended.

All that lingered was Penny's mixed feelings of ecstasy and guilt, peppered with the smallest repulsion.

She was an altogether a normal looking girl. Nineteen years old with light brown hair and hazel eyes. Her build was thick but not overweight. Leftover baby fat that had been evened out by the coming of her adult curves.

She had an altogether normal room that contained nothing at all to give away her strange inclinations. There was a Radiohead poster on her wall. An 'Obama oh-eight' sticker covered a chipped patch of wood on her dresser.

It was peculiar to her. These desires that swam through the back of her mind. It started in high school when a classmate of hers spoke at an assembly. Her name was Chelsea. Penny always knew that Chelsea was easy. She went with guys to the school parking lot to make out in their cars after football games. She had a cold sore once and people said it was the kind that flares up again and again and never goes away.

It was some night right before school let out for summer, that Chelsea was raped. Through tears and sobs, Chelsea told the whole school about how so and so, a student now expelled and awaiting trial, had went to far with her in one of those cars in the parking lot. She acted as though she was coerced into ending up there, as if she had never done it before. She was young, dumb, and naive, but any amount of playful promiscuity on her part did not mean she deserved to be raped, to be violated in the most heinous way imaginable. So even though Chelsea was a bit of a slut, Penny had felt remorse for her, but Penny also felt good. Not only good, but jealous. Here was Chelsea standing petrified on the stage, reliving trauma that made her legs buckle at that very moment. Consumed by sheer terror. And all Penny could think about was how she wanted it. To be completely consumed by another human being. To be stripped of all dignity and humanity. To be destroyed. She fantasized about this night after night.

MESMERISM AND CHLOROFORM OR BAD PENNY MAKES CHANGE

She started researching these feelings on the computer and soon she began dipping into the seediest corners of the web. She stumbled across a video and there it was at last. 'Catharsis'. Those images she saw aroused things in her that she had been trying to reproduce ever since. She knew that such a high could only once again be realized by one thing: Actualization, which of course, meant death itself.

* * *

It was Wednesday night and Penny had gone to see a band with her friend Thalia. The clock was nearing twelve but Penny had no classes the next day so it didn't matter. The band was a droning post-punk outfit. All melodrama and a guitar sound like a chainsaw. And no talent. Some bands could get away with this kind of sound, but this group wasn't one of them. She couldn't even remember their name.

Penny resorted to people watching. Her eyes on the bodies that shifted through the tight sea of flesh. There was a man standing alone. Penny had seen him with a girl earlier but she had vanished. He was average size though muscular, with sun colored hair and a farmer's tan.

"I think that guy is looking at you," said Thalia to Penny.

Penny didn't respond. She walked over to the man.

"Hi," he said with a grin. Penny noticed a chip in his front tooth.

"Hey," bellowed Penny over the chainsaw guitars. "Do you like this band?"

"Not really, no," the man said.

Penny pointed to the exit. "Do you want to-?"

"Yeah. Sure," said the man.

They walked out into an alley behind the venue. Other people were scattered around. Smoking. Talking on cell phones.

"So what's your name?" Penny asked.

"Kevin."

"I'm Penny." She wiped her glasses on her shirt sleeve.

"Would you like to go get a hamburger?" Kevin asked.

"Sure."

Penny sat with Kevin in his rundown Camaro, outside of a fast food restaurant.

"I love these twenty four hour drive throughs," said Kevin before sucking up cheap vanilla soft serve through a straw.

"Me too," said Penny, picking a French fry from the grease stained paper bag and popping it in her mouth. "So," said Penny as she brushed the crumbs from her hands. "What do you want to be when you grow up?"

"I am grown up," said Kevin.

"Well, you know," said Penny, drinking cola from a plastic cup.

"I think I'll go to work for a pharmaceutical company."

"Why?" Penny asked.

"Because medicine is important to people," said Kevin.

"Why not be a doctor?" asked Penny, with a curious glance.

"For what?"

"You could help more people that way."

Kevin shrugged.

Kevin's room was dirty and dull. A typical dwelling for a bachelor, even though the rest of the apartment was clean and tidy. They sat on the foot of his unmade bed.

"So what do you want to do when you grow up?" said Kevin.

Penny's eyes became glazed over as she stared at the wall. "I don't think about the future. I live in the present. You can't hang everything on dreams."

Kevin saw this dazed look in Penny's eyes. "Hey, are you okay?" he asked, brushing the strands of hair from the side of her face.

MESMERISM AND CHLOROFORM OR BAD PENNY MAKES CHANGE

"Yeah, I'm fine," she said with a faint smile.

With a sudden hunger, Kevin pressed his lips hard against Penny's mouth, trying to slip his tongue into the warm moisture of her gullet. She resisted these advances at first, attempting to escape with meek effort, but then she succumbed and opened her mouth.

She felt the buttons of her blouse snap loose and the cool air of a nearby fan against her skin. Kevin's hand was pushing up her black wool skirt, pulling down her underwear, and then pushing her shoulders back.

He was fumbling with his zipper.

"No, don't," said Penny. This could be it, Penny thought.

Something dawned on her then. She didn't want this. To be violated. To be slain. She wanted life as it is. She was content with the way things were. She feared what was to come. She was trembling as his hands held her down. The crystalline tears ran out of her eyes. She tilted her head back, her contorted mouth emitting sounds of suffering.

She saw a small red light on the bookshelf behind her. She saw her face reflected in a small circle of black glass. A smiling face.

"Is that a camera?"

"Shut the fuck up," said Kevin. He did not notice the small hint of pleasure seeping through the fear in Penny's creaking voice.

Consumed with both fear and wonder, she waited for the stinging of his entrance into her virginal womb and it did not come.

Kevin stood up.

What is he doing? thought Penny.

He pulls a quarter from his pocket and flips it.

The coin lands in his open palm, which closes around it as Kevin exhales a breath of what may have been relief.

"What's going on?" asks Penny.

"If it came up heads I was going to do it, but it came up tails. That has to be God intervening. Letting me know it isn't right."

Penny sees an open shoebox on the ground beneath his bed. Inside is a small black pistol. She stares for a long time. Her eyes come alive with a bright fire. Contentment can hold her no longer. Waves surge through her body and give her want. A desperate need for something more. An unexplainable force that demands her transformation.

"But don't you want it?" she asked him, undoing her bra and throwing it to the floor.

"What?" replied Kevin with hesitation.

She lifted her skirt and spread her legs, glaring at him.

He pounced on Penny, splitting her open and starting a fire inside of her. It is pain and pleasure and everything she had ever wanted; every emotion she had ever felt combined and amplified in a nameless surge of power.

She wept from the pain and this drove him on. Her physical hurt that he mistook for reluctance.

"Yes," she muttered. "More!"

He paused for a moment. "Shut up," he said.

"Oh, give me more," she voiced in a loud groan.

"Shut the fuck up you stupid bitch," he growled at her. "They'll hear you."

He isn't alone here after all. He must live with his parents, Penny thought.

He was thrusting with wild force inside of her and sending chills up her spine.

"Oh yes," she moaned loud.

"I said shut up you fucking bitch!" he snapped again.

Without stopping he snatches up the gun from the floor and shoves it in her mouth.

"If you make another sound, I'll shoot you."

She could tell he was bluffing. She wondered if the gun was loaded. She ran her tongue along the cold metal of the barrel and felt a lump form in her throat. A lump that snaked down through her body and caused a numb warmth to form in the deepness of her womb. She knew what was coming. It was time to acknowledge the truth. To take action. To cause the change and allow herself to be free. She resolved herself to it as the orgasm rushed through her body and with a shaking hand she reached up and pulled the trigger. The explosion sounded and all was quiet. The wall was covered in blood. Fireworks of human flesh.

NEXT TIME
Carol Ann M. Van Natten

I'm not even sure why I did it. It's only been a few hours and I can already smell the death of human flesh. Most of this putrid smell was here while he was still living – the body odor of a hobo, who probably doesn't know when he had his last meal, let alone when he had his last shower. Shit stains and urine spots, mixed with blood and decaying flesh. The only clean thing about this forsaken soul was the blood that came from within him.

When it splattered on my hand I was compelled to lick it off and the taste of pennies matched the taste of my own blood. I am reminded of my enjoyment from when I was younger. I would make it flow by my own doing, just to experience the unique flavor.

I started by cutting myself — sliding a sharp knife across the inside of my forearm. The sensation was cold like ice against my skin, but the burn radiated from within my flesh. I realized that pain and pleasure were the same for me. I do not feel pain like others feel it — I close my eyes, roll them back in my head while my nervous system transmits the impulses to my brain, where I turn them into slivers of electric sex with a conscious cognitive thought. This revelation changed my life. My blood lust recognized, my ferocity became clearer to me. New meaning was found in every experience. Casual encounters with strangers became "fucking" instead of "sex" and I ventured into the realms that lead me to places with names like *The Dungeon*. One place in particular held sexual raves, with terrifying and erotic devices that hung on the walls, like bloodletting by whipping. Something that held intrigue to me was where one could hang from hooks that were threaded through the skin of the back.

CAROL ANN M. VAN NATTEN

My first encounter at *The Dungeon*, I was approached by a couple. She was a chubby, round-faced, short, little thing in a school girl plaid skirt, white blouse and stereo-typical pig tails. Her boyfriend wore black leather pants and a black T-shirt that had safety pins holding it together over strategically placed cuts in the fabric. I could see his freckled flesh peeking through one hole and the hint of a hard lickable collarbone through another. Freckles drive me crazy. They invited me to sit with them and I ordered a drink. They were intrigued by my appearance as I had a very unassuming image for this kind of place. I was in a pair of tight dark denim jeans that hugged me so tight that my 5'10" frame looked to be all legs, with a crushed velvet burgundy halter top which accentuated my 44-Ds. With my hair straight down to my ass and wearing little makeup, I looked quite out of place in this pit of faux-goth girls and guys that were indistinguishably metrosexual.

I wanted to fuck and that's why I had come to this deviant gathering of misfits and lurid activities. I was looking for something dirty, quick and exhilarating. I agreed to leave with my new acquaintances as they both had their eye on doing nefarious things to me, which sounded exactly what I was looking for. This threesome thing was old hat to me by this point, but it had been a while since I had gotten any and I was up for whatever got me off. I hadn't expected it to be the next level of my new found revelation, but soon realized that it would not satiate any lust I had, but in fact, amplify it.

The pain was only temporary as the boyfriend wrapped my wrists and ankles with cheap yellow polyester braided rope and tied it in such a manner that any movement on my part tightened its grasp on me. I was clipped to a chain attached to the ceiling. It arched my back towards it with my stomach on the bed. My chest was bare and uplifted, presented toward the head of the bed, where the girl sat and masturbated while watching her man take me from behind. The burning sensation of the rope was exquisite in conjunction with his animalistic thrusts; I found lust and eroticism I had not yet known. When he was about to climax, he grabbed hold of my hair and tugged with all his might, which sent me right to the edge. For some reason, I asked him to grab my throat. I've always held my breath when I cum and I wanted him to control the asphyxiation. When I came, and I came hard releasing all over his cock, I released a darkness I could no longer contain.

I would go to that club, a dive of eroticism, every weekend to try new devices and explore the sexual possibilities as my lusts grew darker and darker and my abilities to satiate them grew harder and harder. Sex was my drug of choice and I amused myself with the thought of just telling someone, *I'll suck your dick if you give me some dick.* I went from being whipped at the club and tasting my own blood, to learning how to whip others in a way that was "just enough" for them — leaving their skin weeping, and yet still enough to appease my lust for control. I experimented with different kinds of asphyxiation on others and loved having others do it to me. It was a release of control, the *idea* of putting my life in someone's hands. I relished the overwhelming power of taking control, of the rush that I felt almost milking the life out of someone else while fucking them, accentuating the French notion of the orgasm as "the little death."

I realized my desires lay outside the realm of sexual eroticism and fetishes when I went home with a young man that I had never seen at the club before. He was a little shorter than me with dark hair, tapered like a military cut and mocha eyes. He had a baby face juxtaposed by a chiseled jaw line that made him resemble Guy Pearce and I wanted to swallow him whole. We got to his place and I saw that it was kind of a dump, with dishes stacked on the counter, a milk-crate under his 12" TV, a shabby flower-print couch and clothes everywhere. There was so much clutter that I barely noticed it was a studio, when in the far right corner I noticed the double bed with plush pillows and a cream-colored down comforter. He apologized for the mess. I told him I didn't care and that he "should see the pigsty I live in," which was a lie because I am a meticulous neat freak and everything has its place.

The night started pretty blasé for my usual intrigues – this kid just needed to get laid. Not a big deal to me really, but with the succubus in a vicious pant inside me, waiting to get out, I started to push the envelope with my new partner. He was up for some "kinky shit" but I had a feeling he was thinking crazy positions — not what I was about to do to him. I was on top, writhing on his cock and clawing at his chest when I slid my hands up to his throat. He didn't stop me so I continued to fuck him, grinding harder and faster until I could tell he was about to blow his load. As he came, I squeezed his throat in my hands and he writhed — flailing in ecstasy. He grabbed my hips and thrust into me harder. I continued squeezing as I came like Cytherea all over his cock and soaked us both. I was so into it and kept gyrating. In my own ecstasy, I hadn't noticed that his hands went limp at my sides until I was done and released my grasp. I looked down at him and noticed he was unconscious. I didn't expect that to happen, but weirdly, didn't care that it did. If anything, I was drunk with the power of the moment and my lust felt satiated. I checked his pulse, he was still alive and breathing; he had only passed out. However, I still thought it best to get the fuck out of dodge.

It was reminiscing about *that* night that I knew I wanted to kill someone. The lust that was burning inside was not physically sexual as others I had felt. It was connected to the desire to kill, to take someone's life, especially with my own two hands. I had to mull this over as I knew that it was not the norm to want to kill someone, but at the same time, I had no moral compass telling me why I shouldn't. I knew from all I'd seen and read that it had to be someone no-one would miss. That way there would be no serious investigation. *I could just make it look like an accident.* But I wanted to kill someone, *brutally* murder them – which would be hard to make look like an accident. Keeping that in mind, I had to choose someone that no-one would care about, or someone they would expect to find murdered. I had thought about a homeless guy, or girl – which might be easier, as there would seemingly be no-one looking for them, and when found, I'd be long gone.

I didn't expect it to be tonight – it just kind of happened. I had been walking down by the factories that line the harbor, casing the homeless population and looking for places to dispose of the body. Up until it happened, I didn't even know if I could go through with it, or if I was just running through a fantasy in my mind. I had brought a bottle of Boone's which I tainted with some Rohypnol, which I was able to score at last night's rave. The plan was to "make nice" with my victim and be able to subdue him or her. I was also armed with the knife that my father had given my brother when he was a teenager for hunting; I have kept it with me ever since his death.I had passed what seemed like all the usual spots that the homeless find to snuggle up to in the chilled air of the night, but continued around the side of a dilapidated factory toward the water's edge. There was a rocky bank down toward the harbor, which was still recovering from the filth the factory had dumped into it years before. I remember being downstream from here when my brother and I were kids and Dad would take us fishing on Sundays.

I was just returning to reality, from my thoughts of a summer day of my youth, when there was a rustling sound behind me. I spun around to find someone getting up from a mound of junk and cloth that was tucked into the huge drainage pipe from the factory. A wiry man, 50-something with salt and pepper matted hair stumbled toward me, moaning in incoherent guttural utterances. As he got closer I could see that he was only in his 40's, but had dirt caked into the crevices of his face and his skin was weather beaten and leathery with years of sun exposure. Without malice, he lurched towards me. I glanced around and saw that we were alone on the bank.

In an instant I decided *it would be him*. I held out the bottle to meet his groping hands. His shocked eyes darted up to mine and I could see the smallest glint of life reflect back at me under the harbor lights. He paused for but a moment, before unscrewing the top and downing half the bottle in what seemed like one gulp. Taking the bottle, he trudged back to his makeshift home. I stared at him wondering how long I would have to stand there and wait for the wine and roofies to sedate him. I wished I had brought my iPod — this was a Tool moment. *"Sober," "Prison Sex"* or *"Vicarious"* would be perfect right now … next time. He continued to drink and held fast to that bottle as though it were his life line. I knew it was just the opposite.

For twenty minutes I watched as he polished off the bottle and organized his belongings of black plastic garbage bags, rummaging through old clothes and blankets stained with shit from humans, birds, and rats — God knows what else. I didn't feel bad for him, nor did I think I was doing him a favor. I was just doing it — for me. When his motions slowed and he sat on the edge of the pipe for a few minutes without moving or moaning, I knew it was about time. He got up and started to move towards me again and stumbled down to one knee. I took the opportunity to get the upper hand and moved to the rock behind him. I practiced a blood choke on him with my right elbow, trying to set it in, under his chin. He began to flail, but he was too weak. This was like nothing I had ever felt before and I loved it. The unwarranted vengeance that coursed through my veins while I was trying to choke this man out was exhilarating. I was in complete control and I was high with lust. It felt better than any amount of fucking I had ever done.

My left hand stopped pressing my right wrist and slid into my back pocket and took out the knife. In an instant it was in his mid-back to the hilt. I could hear the air escape the lung I punctured and a baby's whimper escape his lips. He started choking on his own blood and coughing it out all over. Pink frothy sputum followed. I grabbed the back of his matted hair with my left hand, released my choke hold on him and removed the knife with my right hand and went straight for his throat. I was blind with rage and ecstasy and was moving through these motions as though it were muscle memory from a past life. My blade only caught for a moment, on cricoid cartilage, as I pressed harder than I thought I had to, in order to penetrate his throat. His body went limp and I let it drop before me. I stood there for a minute or two, just staring at the blood staining the rocks under him as his reflexes jerked his body and his arterial blood flow stopped. I tilted my head to the sky, closed my eyes, held my breath and felt the rush. A moan caught in my throat, which left my mouth, and I began to breathe heavily. I could feel how wet I had gotten. I savored the moment, and relaxed my breathing as I gazed at the night sky. I sat down beside him and my mind was blank for quite some time.

I did it; I killed a man. Me, a statuesque woman of twenty-seven, with a past that no-one cares about, least of all me. Most of it is locked away in the padded brain-cells of my mind anyway. I have no regret over what I have just done, outside of my disappointment that I made such a mess and several mistakes. *I shouldn't have worn my favorite jeans.* Lesson learned. *I have to work on approach ... and my timing, and tweak the way I start my attack.* Other than that, there is no residual feeling, beyond satisfaction. No right, no wrong. Maybe I would have liked him to fight more.

I'll have to experiment with that ... next time.

NIGHT LIFE
Michael Matheson

Kelly Kenney and I cross the bridge over to Jefferson, past the trolley tracks, her heels clip-tripping on the raised lines. Sweet Kelly Kenney. Legs down to there and tits up to here. Doesn't know the meaning of the word no. My kind of girl.

Hubert likes her too. Hell, he's practically humping my shoulder with the taste of her whetting the air. His long gammy shanks ride up my forearm on one side and my left shoulder blade on the other. His double-jointed arms curl around my throat and one hand slides down to my solar plexus suggestively. His priapic phallus digs its way into my right shoulder as he nibbles on my earlobe.

"Maybe we can both take this one," Hubert whispers kitten soft into my ear. His breath reeks of Jack Daniels and urine, and the brush of his lips on the pale, short hairs on my outer ear is the creak and rustle of old leather.

I smile down at Kelly and she smiles back, sort of sidles up close and snuggles in as we walk – a cold November wind biting at skin and bone beneath, coats be damned.

Hubert cops a feel and Kelly smiles up at me thinking it's my hand. "Oh how soft she is," his hoary rasp tickles in my ear. "Think of what we could do with the pretty pretty," he goads, his swollen member throbbing hot against my back.

The wind tears at my overcoat, setting Hubert fluttering like a dried leaf and he digs his claws deep into my arms, winding his tail in several coils around the arm Kelly's dangling from. I don't think she notices Hubert's tail. I don't think she can see him at all. That's good. Makes it easier.

Kelly shivers as we walk, the streets mostly empty in the chill autumn evening. It's hardly surprising – she's wearing a fleet cut coat, open at the breast and the wind keeps whipping its edges away from her legs. Her skirt isn't just mini, it's practically nonexistent, and if she's wearing underwear – above or below – I haven't seen any sign of it. All standard fare for the strobing, noisy, sweat-soaked club where I found her, but it's no match for the biting autumnal cold. She wraps herself around me, huddling in against the chill and I get a flood of a different kind of heat than the never ending pulse of Hubert's engorged, veiny prick. But he's right. She is soft.

The crowds thin out as we pass under the El, the cars rattling by like sustained thunder. Their echo reverberates against the cracked macadam, setting my teeth on edge.

"Not far now," whispers Kelly into my ear, her hot breath misting as it rolls around the tender flesh. "I live just down the end of the block."

Hubert leans in to sniff at her hair, flattened ape-like nostrils flaring as he drinks her in. I shift my shoulders to redistribute his weight as he convulses in pure pleasure, eyes closed.

"Cold's not getting to you, is it?" Kelly asks my neck, sliding a not so subtle hand down behind the front lip of my jeans. "Mmm, still warm where it counts," she moans, nuzzling my neck with her nose and her lips, brushing her tongue on the side of my Adam's apple as we come in sight of her tenement. Hubert is apoplectic, twitching at my back, his claws digging gouges in the soft meat of my arms as we come up to the building's outer door.

She stops fumbling with me long enough to fumble for her keys, and then we're through the outer door and the rundown lobby – faded posters on the walls and blinking fluorescents overhead – and into the elevator.

The ride up is long. She guides my hand between her thighs and pulls my head in against the hollow of her neck as Hubert watches, panting. She whimpers, head thrown back as I work my tongue over the side of her neck, Hubert doing likewise for the other.

114

NIGHT LIFE

By the time we get to her apartment door, her coat is trailing behind her, hanging from one wrist and her shirt is riding down off her shoulders. I'm right, she isn't wearing any underwear. Her nipples are hard and erect beneath my cupping palm and flicking fingers. Her tongue insinuates itself into my mouth as she slams the door of her apartment shut. She sucks the air out of my lungs, one calf up around my hip and arched taut over my buttock as she shucks the rest of her clothes off. She reaches up to cup my cheek with one hand as she tugs at my belt with the other, drawing back from the kiss, as I throw her to the floor and stretch.

"What the fuck?" she growls up at me, her limbs splayed and her clothes hanging like tattered tarps off her half-naked body while she rises to her elbows, murder in her eyes.

"You got a fridge in this place?" I ask, rubbernecking. She must have one somewhere. Everyone does, right? I mean even if it's just an icebox everybody's got one, even in a shithole like this.

She goggles, breathing hard, her sweat-plaited hair hanging down in wet streamers across her face.

I find the fridge with an "ah", making my way over and rooting around as Hubert ogles her exposed curves, breathing hard and fast. His straining phallus beats on the air like a drum. I dig out her milk carton – skim, oh well – and toss it back as Hubert shifts position on my back, his leathery scales brushing up against the exposed skin at the back of my neck as he pivots and tenses.

"Are you fuc -" Kelly spits, interrupted as Hubert springs and lands on top of her, pinning her beneath his substantial weight. Her eyes scrabble for purchase on the empty air above her as she kicks out with both legs. Hubert clamps his claws on her wrists and pushes her down, running his sandpaper tongue over her neck. Kelly struggles beneath him, legs fan kicking until Hubert pins her legs with his own, then uses his whole body to flatten her against the floor. He's hungry in every sense of the word, and he indulges himself slowly.

Kelly's beautiful falsetto screaming rips through the apartment, and out the open window, tearing at the cold wind blowing outside.

You've gotta love a girl who can't say no.

SAFE SEX
Trey Dowell

They had a perfectly functional sex life for three years before things started to go bad.

It began harmlessly enough: a simple statement at the dinner table.

"I think we should start trying," she said, lowering her book to peer at him over her reading glasses.

He let the spoonful of mashed potatoes reach his mouth before mumbling, "Trr frr whut?"

"To have a baby, silly."

He choked on the lump of potatoes halfway down his esophagus, brain sending an emergency signal to lurch for his milk. He didn't want to look panicked—it sent the wrong message—but mashed potatoes exiting through your nostrils sent up some disturbing red flags too. A cool swig of milk soothed his throat plus gave him three seconds to think up an explanation for the reaction.

"You okay there, big boy?"

"Yeah! Sorry about that … fully aware how bad it looks, but honest, I'm just surprised! Of course I think it's a great idea … I've been begging you for months."

A skeptical corner of her mouth pursed. "I remember a lot of begging to get rid of the condoms. Don't recall hearing the word 'baby' in those conversations much."

He wished he had another bite of potatoes queued up. The precious seconds to formulate a response would have been handy. Sadly, no spoonful of respite waited, so he went with his gut. "I *always* wanted to be a father, and more importantly, I can't think of another woman in the world I'd rather be a parent with."

P.S. No condoms, he added mentally.

117

She, as was her custom, heard both sentences. She snickered at his transparency and returned to reading while picking at her plate.

He thought for a moment, took a long look around the room, and exaggerated an exhale. "So, when you say *try*, were you thinking about, y'know, next week? Or …"

"Tonight, sweetie. I was thinking about starting tonight."

He, as was his custom, pumped his fist below the table.

She smiled.

* * *

When the time for the first attempt arrived, it was met by two vastly different levels of anticipation. She went through her normal pre-bedtime ritual; a 15-minute process involving clothing removal, bathroom break, face wash, teeth brushing, and dental floss. He was naked and under the covers in 15 seconds.

Fourteen minutes and forty-five seconds later, she came out of the bathroom in flannel pajamas, world-renowned in the married-sex-life business as the 'hands-off' clothing choice. His dismay at her sleepwear evident, she reassured him as she crawled into bed.

"Don't worry, horndog. They come off."

His look of unexpected good fortune returned and he ran his hand over the soft flannel above her hip. "Not exactly the romantic feel I pictured for such an auspicious event," he said.

"Um, do you want romance? Or sex?"

He reached for her in earnest, saying, "Question asked, question answered."

To no one's surprise, the evening's entertainment was better (and briefer) than normal.

SAFE SEX

He woke up lying on his side, to the startling image of open eyes just inches from his own.

He recoiled, then immediately regretted the overreaction: cringing from your wife's face is seldom a wise decision. Best follow-up strategy? Shameless flattery.

"Hi there, gorgeous," he whispered.

No response. The eyes kept boring into his own - unblinking, unmoving. A second of panic in his chest, then relief: he could see her ribcage rising and falling with each deep breath.

"Honey? Are you okay?"

Again, nothing.

Was she sleeping with her eyes open? He'd heard of such a thing, but never witnessed it. He lifted a hand from beneath the covers and reached to touch her shoulder. Halfway to target, the hand stopped.

Movement.

Only the eyes, not the head. Her pupils had followed his hand as it came toward her. Now they focused on the levitating fingers, less than a foot from her shoulder. On impulse, he drew the hand back across her field of vision, then up, then down. Her eyes tracked every inch of slow motion.

"Whoa. Creepy." His unease did not, however, prevent him from drawing looping figure eights in the air, and watching her eyes dance.

After growing tired of the game, he stopped and his hand reached the original target. He shook her lightly, saying her name in soft syllables. Her eyes blinked, darted in several directions, then refocused on him.

"What ... what's going on? "she stammered.

"Nothing. You were sleeping with your eyes open. I just wanted to make sure you were okay."

Her brow scrunched. "What? Nobody does that. Go back to sleep, weirdo." She closed her eyes and in moments, did exactly that. He joined her. After flipping over to face the night table. Like most things which happen at 3:30 AM, the incident was quickly forgotten.

* * *

The next morning presented a complete role reversal. A self-described morning person, he yawned and grumbled all the way to the coffee maker.

She, meanwhile, traded in her normally sullen dragging body, for the energy of a six-year-old on Saturday morning. She flitted like a hummingbird around the kitchen, spooning scrambled eggs and cheese on plates and sliding them to the table. She looked at his T-shirt and boxers with displeasure. "You're gonna be late. Get dressed, mister!"

"Good Lord, what got into you?" his mouth said, below squinting, sleepy eyes.

She walked over and greeted him with a much longer kiss than normal and to his happy surprise, a hand between his legs. "You did, apparently." She pivoted and walked back to the sink, and he noticed the extra butt-shake in her stride. This, from a woman, who usually couldn't be bothered with a peck on the cheek before staggering to her car in the morning.

He was entranced, watching her in her business clothes, skirt tight against her hips. He almost suggested a second baby-making attempt, right there in the kitchen, preferably on the table while half-clothed, but decided against it. Felt wrong, like it would break the spell somehow — and more than anything, he wanted to maintain this Twilight-Zone sense of passionate enchantment for as long as possible.

When they said goodbye in the driveway before heading to their cars, the heat level of the kiss officially qualified as gratuitous PDA.

"Tonight?" he said.

Her hand explored his crotch once more, and its target was not difficult to find. An urgent rub and squeeze later, she pulled away and walked around to the driver's side of her car. Before ducking down into the vehicle, she bit her lower lip and threw him her best salacious grin.

Question asked, question answered.

* * *

Twenty-six text messages zipped between their phones that day, and not a single one involved schedules, shopping lists, or the checking account. All twenty-six messages had titillating imagery, twenty-one mentioned various body parts, and fifteen used language entirely inappropriate for work-supplied smart phones. Her best text had a picture attached which made him spew Diet Dr. Pepper all over his keyboard.

They both left work early.

Their arrival home was more Olympic Event than polite reunion. Baby-Making Attempt number two started in the foyer, and spread up the steps of their split-level home to the living room. Attempt number three happened roughly twenty minutes after the conclusion of number two, still on the floor of the living room, still with both athletes partially in uniform. After a necessary dinner break to rest and refuel, attempt number four finally saw them achieve both nakedness and the bedroom. By ten o'clock, both participants realized that without the use of intravenous fluids and industrial lubricant, it was time to stop.

"My God," he said, sweaty body collapsing against the cool sheets next to her. "What's happened to us?"

She giggled.

He looked first at her, then the ceiling in disbelief. "I thought I knew what good sex was. I've never been so happy to be so wrong."

"There is nothing wrong about what we just did," she purred.

"Three times!" The serene satisfaction in his voice was evident.

"Three times for you, Marathon Man. My number was a lot higher."

He twisted his head to look at her. "How much higher?"

"You are such a guy." She silenced further questions by wrapping a leg over him and sliding her body against his contours. He reached over to the night table with his free arm and flicked the lamp switch.

"If raising a baby is half as much fun as creating one, I am seriously going to enjoy being a father. I mean, *seriously*," he said in the darkened room.

Her head nestled against his chest. "You are so cute sometimes, I could just eat you up."

Within moments, they were asleep.

2:47 A.M.

When he opened his eyes, he saw the green numbers flashing on the bedside alarm clock. Power failure, now restored, but it meant the alarm wouldn't activate unless reset. He fumbled in the dark for the buttons, mumbling curse words until finally the numbers stopped flashing and the confirmation beep of the alarm sounded. He rolled over to check on her and cried out in surprise.

She sat fully upright, torso twisted toward him. Her face illuminated in the pale green light of the clock, eyes open, watching.

"What the hell?" He sounded irritated, but irritation wasn't the emotion making his heart pound. His chest thumped like an anvil taking rapid blows from a blacksmith's hammer.

Memory of last night's odd awakening flooded back. He rose to look at her face-to-face, and when he did, his own body blocked the alarm clock. The ghostly light evaporated, leaving her face in silhouette. He took her shoulders in hand, expecting them to be soft and compliant in her physical state—but they weren't. Her body felt taut, strong—poised. When she wouldn't respond to gentle rubbing he shook her shoulders with increasing strength, eventually hard enough to make her head bobble.

Just like the previous night, she came around, oblivious to his concern. "What … what are you doing?" she said.

"Waking you up," he said with relief. "You were sitting straight up in bed … sleeping with your eyes open. You did it last night too. Don't you remember?"

She hesitated, confused. "I … I don't know …"

"Just lie down. Go back to sleep. We can talk about it in the morning." He guided her down to the sheets, then took his place beside her. Sleep was slow to come this time. He lay on his back, stealing furtive glances to the left, checking …

There was almost no room between him and the edge of the mattress.

* * *

No mention of the sleeping problems the next morning.

She was just as vivacious as the day before, but he was dragging even worse which kept conversation to a minimum. In addition, he was paying the price of copious lovemaking: feeling as though someone took a belt sander to his private parts.

"Hon, I think I'm gonna be out of action for a couple of days on the baby-making front," he said before walking out the door. "You practically killed me last night. Plus, I feel like I've got a cold coming on … not myself this morning."

"Not a big deal, sweetie. Take a sick day if you need to—I want you back in fighting shape as soon as possible."

"Aye aye, Cap'n!" he said with a smile and a salute before closing the door behind him.

The smile was gone before he cleared the porch.

* * *

Google. WebMD. Bing.

From his work computer, he'd looked up every variety of sleepwalking he could find.

Nothing.

No disorder involving sitting upright while asleep, eyes completely open and body rigid. In frustration, he went back to Google and typed a string of words, looking for any commonality the search engine could find. WOMAN, NIGHT, SLEEP, EYES, SEX, SICKNESS—all went in the search box. Most of what came back was useless: jokes, advertisements for sleep aids, and a pornographic movie review.

Halfway down the page, though, was a word he didn't recognize. Clicking on the link brought the dreaded "Unauthorized Website Traffic Blocked" page from his corporate server. Yet another black mark in the personnel file.

Undaunted, he lobbed his voice over the cubicle wall. "Barry? You there?"

"Yep."

"You ever hear the word 'succubus'?"

He heard Barry's chair roll as the big man launched himself around the corner, a seat-bound cruise-missile.

"Dude, are you lookin' at porn?"

"No! Keep your voice down … God, why would you even ask me that?"

"Hey, you're the one asking about a succubus. Didn't you ever read any fantasy stuff in high school?"

"What, like Dungeons and Dragons? No. Why? What is it?"

"A succubus is like, an erotic demon-woman or something. They seduce men, feed on their vitality—their, well, y'know …"

"Their what?"

"Their *stuff!*" Barry said, pointing to his crotch. "Why do you wanna know?"

Their voices grew quiet between the cubicle walls as private details were exchanged. He told Barry about the sleepwalking—more like sleep stalking Barry offered—along with the fevered attempts to conceive, hotter and different than their sex life had ever been.

When he was finished, he looked for answers in Barry's dumbstruck face. "Well? What do you think?"

"One question. Before you guys decided to have the baby, did you ever … y'know … *inside* her?"

"No. She had a bad experience with birth control pills in high school. Something with her thyroid. We've always used condoms."

Barry nodded with authority. "Okay then, no question. She's a succubus."

"WHAT?"

Barry thrust a finger to shushed lips. "Jesus! Be quiet, will ya? I'm screwing with you, you idiot. Listen—I've known Lily almost as long as you have. She goes to church. She loves scrapbooking. She made a seating chart for your 32nd birthday dinner, for Christ's sake! No way is that chick a demon."

He chuckled at the absurdity. "Yeah. I'm just being paranoid, right?" He paused. "What should I do? Talk to her about it?"

Barry laughed. "And violate marital custom? Go with my policy: avoid problems until they bite you in the ass."

He managed a weak smile. Barry gave him a quick look-over. "You want my advice? Go home. You look like hell. And until Lily starts juggling knives in her sleep, if she's generous enough to want sex with a loser like you—be smart and say 'Yes, please'!"

* * *

His cold lasted three days.

The first night was hellish. Mixing a fever with expectations of sleep-stalking did little for his ability to relax. She woke once, to find him sweaty and fully awake.

"Why don't you take some Nyquil? That stuff makes you dead to the world."

He imagined her staring at his unconscious body, then moving closer as his defenseless drug-addled form offered no resistance beyond snoring.

"Nah. I'm good."

"Suit yourself, sickie," she said, before rolling away and pulling the covers tight over her shoulder.

In spite of the hours of rotating chills, sweats, and watchful vigilance, when dawn came he greeted it with a smile. No unusual behavior. No three AM surprises.

He napped, but only after she left for work.

The fever didn't break by the second day, so he slept in the guest bedroom at her urging. The solitude allowed him to relent on the Nyquil. It was his most restful night in a week.

"How you feeling?" she said before leaving for work on day three.

"Better. If you don't mind though, I think I'll sleep one more night in the guest bed. I can thrash around and not bother you."

She frowned. "I like having you next to me. One more night, but that's it, deal?"

He nodded with a smile. "Absolutely."

"And not to give you any incentive or anything, but I checked the math and I should be ovulating the next couple of days … in case you're interested."

It took a lot of effort, but his smile stayed in place. "I'm gonna stay home one more day to rest up, then."

"Smart boy …" She unfastened the top button of her blouse and winked before heading to the door.

* * *

Third day was better, but he wasn't operating at full-speed yet.

"Still got a bit of a fever, sweetie. Rain check on the baby-making?" he said over dinner.

Her frown graduated to a full pout. "Dammit! Stupid cold. If you feel like this again tomorrow, I'm calling Dr. Bloomberg."

"If I feel like this for another day, trust me, I'll call him myself."

She twisted her fork in a plate of linguine. "Shame, really, because I was looking forward to tonight. Even did something special for you."

"Really? What?"

She kept twirling the fork, spinning a tremendous spool of pasta.

"Let's just say the playing field is clear. Smooth, as it were."

Even sick, he felt a spasm from beneath the table.

"Oh damn," he breathed.

She grinned. "Get well soon."

* * *

That night, she came to him.

She slipped her naked body under the covers, straddling him with cool, strong thighs. When he began to protest, she touched a finger to his lips. "Shhh, it's okay. You lay back, I'll do all the work."

Her smooth skin slid over his body, and he luxuriated in the sensation. She kissed him and he buried his hands in her hair. "Three days is too long," she whispered in his ear.

The thick embrace of her scent and her warmth destroyed any hesitation. Thoughts of sleep aberrations and nocturnal stalking faded away. All that was left was her.

"I'll show you too long," he said, rolling her underneath

him.

And he did.

When they were finished, she stayed only long enough to cool down. She kissed him lightly on the lips and went back to the master bed, leaving him to a solitary, well-earned night of sleep.

3:45 A.M.

A blast of thunder woke him. His eyes snapped open and he heard white noise cut off. The router, air conditioning, and ceiling fan suffered simultaneous deaths. He grumbled in frustration with the power failure and wondered how bad the storm was. He sat up to look out the picture window across the room and immediately came unglued.

"Holy shit!" he yelled, limbs scrambling like a bug on water to push him upright against the headboard.

She stood at the foot of the bed, a statue silhouetted in the dark by staccato bursts of lightning.

"Goddammit, are you awake?" he demanded, breaths coming fast.

No response from the statue, clothed only in a sheer negligee. He saw lightning flashes through the gossamer fabric, highlighting an hourglass shape.

"Honey! Snap out of it!"

Continued silence. He couldn't make out facial features, but he knew the eyes had to be open, watching. In a rare burst of anger, he ripped the top sheet away from his body and slid off the side of the bed. Drawn to full height, he sucked in a breath and moved to grab her—but each step closer, his resolve withered.

Her gaze *followed* him.

The silent figure rotated from the neck only, watching his approach. His steps slowed, reluctant as he drew near. He stopped three feet from her. Now up close, he saw her face;

emotionless, eyes wide.

Bravado now sapped by fear, he whispered. "Baby, please … please wake up."

Instinctively, he reached toward her hand. Shock almost caused him to jump back when he saw her fingers move toward his own. He stopped, and she mimicked him; their open hands frozen in midair within inches. Seconds stretched and peals of thunder made the walls and floor vibrate, but he couldn't take his eyes from her. She looked so awake, so in control … yet totally detached. Finally, he forced his hand to move across the distance and grasp hers. She didn't resist — the grip was cool, light.

He didn't shake her awake this time … the idea of getting any closer stole his will completely. He pulled her from the room and she followed easily, dark eyes peering at him from beneath a lowered brow. He led her back to their room and eased her into bed. Even tucked in, the solitary gaze never left him.

When he returned to the guest bedroom, he locked the door behind him. Under the sheets, his body shivered. For the first time in his life, he hoped he was feverish. An hour later, he finally succumbed to a fitful sleep plagued with restlessness and bad dreams.

He never saw the doorknob slowly twisting back and forth, back and forth … the door pushing inward against the jamb. The quiet squeaks of the knob drowned in the constant patter of the rain outside. They lasted for more than an hour.

The lock held.

* * *

He told her everything. He was too frightened not to.

They sat in the kitchen and he replayed the entire scene from the previous night. To her credit, she listened without interruption or becoming defensive. Her disbelief, however, was impossible to hide. "You've been sick and feverish for days, sweetie. Are you sure it wasn't some kind of dream or hallucination?"

"No. Trust me, it happened," he said, resolve firm. "I didn't dream up the power outage." He pointed over her shoulder at the flashing numbers on the microwave.

She grasped his hand on the kitchen table. "I believe you."

He saw in her eyes she didn't; not really. She loved him and he needed her to believe, so she said she did. It was who she was—one of the reasons he married her. But as much as he loved those deep brown eyes when they focused on him in the daylight, he now feared them at night. And not every night, he suddenly realized.

Only when we have sex, he thought.

He was still turning it over in his mind when she patted and released his hand.

"It's decided. I'll call Dr. Bloomberg today and get a referral to a sleep clinic. What do you think?"

He nodded and smiled, but barely heard any of the words. He was too busy thinking about Barry and his erotic demon-woman.

* * *

"Are you serious?" Barry said when the story was repeated.

"Happened just like I said. Freaked me out. Messed up, right?"

Barry looked unsteady. "Y'know I was just kidding with all the succubus stuff, right?"

"Yeah, I know. But it's a lot less funny now. I sure as hell wasn't laughing when I woke up and saw her standing there."

"I would've shit the bed," Barry confessed.

"She said something about a sleep clinic. Maybe that'll help."

"And the crazy stalker stuff only happens on the nights

when you have sex?"

"So far, yeah. What the hell am I gonna do?"

Barry nodded and thought for a moment. "Hope the clinic has some answers, I guess. In the meantime ... I'd stop fuckin' her."

"Thanks, genius."

* * *

He took Barry's advice. No sex. No late night surprises.

At first, he was delighted. After a week though, delight turned to bewilderment. In two weeks, bewilderment gave way to worry. After three, the only emotion left was despair.

Barry eventually noticed his despondency and the big man pulled him into an empty conference room. "How much longer until the clinic appointment?"

"Sleep problems are apparently an epidemic. Clinic was booked a month in advance, so we've still got another week to go."

"Man, you look terrible. I thought the sleep stalking was on hiatus. What's the problem?"

He pulled in opposite directions: on one side, he was dying to tell someone ... anyone. But on the other side ... the unreality, the craziness of the last few weeks. He imagined it might all still be an illusion, but if he gave it voice—described it out loud—it could somehow become real.

"You wouldn't believe me if I told you."

"C'mon! You cannot introduce something that way and keep it to yourself," Barry whined.

He ran his hands through his hair and plopped into one of the armchairs surrounding the table. "She's *changing*."

Barry sat down in a chair next to him. "What do you mean?"

The words started rolling out, and once started, they were impossible to stop. "I thought everything was fine. I told her we should stop the baby stuff until her appointment … told her the problems only seem to happen when we have sex, right? And she was totally okay with it! She said no problem, it's only a month. 'Your loss', she told me … but she was laughing when she said it. I swear, she was really alright with the whole thing."

"So you stopped. I knew that already. What happened next?"

"At first I thought I was imagining things; maybe it was trick of the lighting, a good angle, anything. She started dressing sexier, showing more cleavage—it was impossible not to notice."

Barry fidgeted in his seat. "Notice *what?*"

"Her boobs got bigger. A lot bigger. To the point where none of her bras fit. Every shirt she owns was skin-tight against her chest. She didn't say a word about it either, just went out and bought bigger sizes. A week later, she had to replace those too!"

Barry shook his head. "Dude! She's probably pregnant. Happens to all of them."

"No. She had her period last week. And before you start talking about hormones or Wonderbras, don't bother. None of that crap makes a woman gain two cup sizes in a week. And that's not all. Her hair grew fast. REAL fast. In three weeks, it's gone from shoulder-length down to the middle of her back."

"Pre-natal vitamins make hair grow faster. It happened to my wife too."

"Dammit, Barry! Pre-natal vitamins help a little. They don't turn a regular woman into goddamn Rapunzel!"

Barry raised his hands in surrender. "Okay, okay … settle down, man."

"And now that she has this beautiful mane of hair, she flaunts it, just like the boobs. She drops stuff all the time, right in front of me. Bends over, shows me gaping cleavage, then flings the hair back over her shoulders as she stands up. Like she's showing off."

Barry drummed his fingers on the hard wood of the table. "God. How horrible for you."

He was oblivious to the skepticism. "But now it's gone even further than that."

"What do you mean?"

"Other parts of her are different too. Her butt is getting bigger. Rounder."

Barry slapped his palm on the table. "Well then send my wife to the sleep clinic too, because that's been happening to her for the last six years!"

"Hysterical. This is different. The same time her ass is getting bigger, her waist is getting smaller. Ever hear of that, funny man? With the boobs and the butt, she's easily put on ten pounds in the last three weeks and her dress size has gone DOWN. That's impossible. Nobody puts on weight and gets a smaller waist."

Barry looked like a dog that'd just had his treat taken away. "Lemme get this straight ... your big problem, the reason you're so depressed ... is because your wife—who desperately wants to have your children—is slowly changing into the girlie silhouette you see on the mudflaps of 18-wheelers?"

He raised his hands in frustration. "Don't you get it? This isn't like having minor cosmetic surgery or getting back into shape. Her entire body is changing ... adapting ... all by itself—in direct response to me NOT having sex with her. It's like she's ..." His voice trailed away.

"Like she's what?" Barry said.

He finally uttered the word he'd been frightened of all along. "Evolving." He slumped in the chair. "It's as if her body wants the sex—needs it—so badly, that it can alter itself to be more sexually attractive ..."

"Okay, Crazy Train, I've heard enough. Lack of sex is starting to affect your brain."

He waved him off. "Her personality is still the same ...

she's still my Lily. We joke around, we watch movies, make dinner. But the physical changes, man … they creep me out and turn me on! I had a hard enough time keeping my hands off of her before all of this happened, and now it's like I sleep next to an uber-pornstar version of my wife. Every time I think about touching her, I remember her standing at the foot of my bed. She was worse than creepy, Barry. She looked dangerous. And it gets worse each time we have sex."

He got up and walked to the window, staring at the cars in the parking lot. "You have any idea what it's like to be wildly turned on and scared shitless at the same time?"

"Every time I go to a strip club, man."

"Be serious."

Barry rose from his chair and walked to the door. "I am serious. You need to snap out of this bullshit. Every guy in the world would die to have your problem." The big man mocked his somber tone. "Oooh, my life is terrible! My super-hot wife wants me! My Ferrari needs gas and my penis is too big for my underwear!"

Barry grumbled as he walked away, leaving the loneliest man on the planet to wonder if he could survive one more night of sex with his super-hot wife.

* * *

She always kept the bathroom door closed, with one exception. Squatting on the toilet, flossing, shaving—all hidden behind six-paneled wood—but when the Jergen's bottle came out, the door swung wide.

Lotion time: the best and worst two minutes of his day.

He tried to read in bed, keep his head focused on the page, but inevitably his gaze drifted back to the bathroom. She stood naked—always naked now—one leg propped on the seat cover, slowly massaging the creamy lotion along each thigh and calf. Her hair obscured her face as she bent down, only to be thrown high as she switched legs, the dark locks flinging around to cascade down her back.

He suffered small doses of torture in his glimpses: the calf muscles pulsing when she flexed up on her toes, hands stroking the cream against her skin until moist thighs gleamed under the bathroom light, eager fingers exploring every square inch of her legs and arms.

By the time she came to bed, his book was a protective tent over his lower regions, hiding his desire. Of course, rather than walk around to her side of the bed, she chose to climb over him, her glorious nudity staring him down in a contest of wills.

She paused above him in the straddle position, breasts pushing into his flannel pajama top. "Wanna fool around?"

The scent of her hair and the lilac of the lotion surrounded him in a sensual cloud.

Oh God, yes.

"C'mon … only one more week until your appointment. Let's be safe."

Her face was playful. "You know, if I didn't know better, I'd think you were afraid of me."

He twisted into an overcompensating mask of incredulity. "What? Don't be silly. I can totally take you."

"That's kind of what I had in mind."

He looked into her brown eyes and flashed back to the night of the storm … her head following him, her hand reaching out to take his. The images allowed him to step back from the cliff's edge. "I'm really tired. Let's just call it a night."

She squinted for an instant, doubting his resolve, but rolled off harmlessly to his left. "Suit yourself." No animosity in her voice, only simple acceptance.

He turned the light off and exhaled in the dark, feeling as though he'd just dodged an incredibly hot bullet.

12:15 A.M.

He awoke to find her mouth on him.

The sheets pulled back, his flannel bottoms pulled down to his knees, her head moving up and down, working him into a hardened frenzy.

"Wait ... what ... what are you doing?"

His protests feeble, she quickened the pace — then stopped to sweep her hair back and laugh at him. "I think you know."

She slinked her way up to his chest, unbuttoning the pajama top and kissing his stomach and chest as she went. When she arrived at his face, she saw his nervousness and immediately swatted it away. "I love you. I would never hurt you, don't you know that?" She whispered in his ear between kisses of his neck. "Make love to me. I need you. Give it to me."

Her hips moved backward and she sat upright in the dim light of the clock. The motion ground her pelvis against his groin, causing him to wince. The brief burst of pain warned him, gave him a second of clarity: *it's not too late to stop.* He heard the warning, but vision overwhelmed hearing — and all he could see was her.

Gorgeous. Eyes wide with excitement, lips full and wet. Hips rocking slowly against his erection in anticipation. Massaging her own impossibly large breasts, then rolling her head in a wide circle, causing her hair to dance over the contours of her shoulders and arms — a waterfall of soft darkness.

His hands moved to her tiny waist. The skin soft, warm. She threw her head back and moaned, "Take me."

Whatever remained of his good sense made a final stand. In between eye blinks: a brief image of a demonic seductress, feeding, using his essence to set her free, flashed over his consciousness. One word in his mind, repeated over and over.

Stopstopstopstopstop.

Then his eyes opened. She lifted her hips slightly, poised

136

to accept him. She was waiting for him, he realized. It had to be his choice. When he hesitated, she took one of her breasts and lifted it to her mouth, teasing the nipple hard with flicks of her tongue.

The act plunged a sharp, final spear through the heart of his resolve. The living embodiment of desire perched above his hips, begging for him to be inside her, was too much.

She rode him to climax, fiery gaze rotating between him and the ceiling. Saliva made her teeth glisten in the haunting green light. She pounded down upon him, repeated demands of "feed me" doing nothing to slow his building eruption. The reptilian part of his brain was in charge now; no thought, no conscience. Like all men drowning in desire, the only actions still under his control were seeing and feeling.

When he came, she screamed.

Collapsed in a heap, the two lovers nuzzled each other, limbs sliding over the thin patina of sweat covering them both. There, in the rare moment completely unclouded by passion, his conscience pulled the bloody spear out of his resolve and tossed it to the ground with disgust.

You're a dead man.

She, as was her custom, heard the unspoken fear and drew her lips to his ear. "Don't worry. I'll lie in your arms all night. You're safe with me."

He believed her.

3:33 A.M.

The rhythmic music of deep breathing rolled across their bedroom, but it was a solo performance. Eyes blinked open in the dark, focused on his defenseless body—warm, inviting. The pulsing jugular, close to her nuzzling face, was so easy.

For the second time that night, he woke up with her mouth on him.

This time, he woke up screaming.

Strong arms pinned him to wet sheets. A mass of dark hair obscured his vision. The frenzied, hungry mouth bit deep and clawed at his throat. He wasn't conscious long, but he did have time to hear the guttural voice, filling the air around him. "Safewithme ... safewithme ... safewithme", the voice hissed. It cackled as the final vestiges of life drained from his body. The last thing he felt were the teeth again—digging, pulling ... tearing.

She fed for a long time, the wet, ripping sounds echoing down the hall of their home. The feast was marvelous, but important as well.

She was, after all, eating for two.

THE CURE
M.Ð. Maurice

Elson was conscious of the hollow tip-tapping noise her sti-letto boot heels made on the shiny tile as she crossed the floor. She was also conscious of the men watching her, in that open and deliberately confident way men in packs do. The attention gave her that same light, heady feeling that having too many glasses of cheap white wine did. Reaching the high lunch counter, Elson flashed a smile at the mousy girl behind it and placed her order while she watched the men out of the corner of her eye. The man on the outskirts of the pack had a griz-zled, hungry appearance that she liked very much. He looked to be older than the others, perhaps a foreman or supervisor. The idea that he was the one with the authority over the others excited her more, *an Alpha male,* she thought, nearly laughing out loud.

In a few moments, her order was handed over the counter and she took it, risking a full look as she bent and transferred it into her bag. He was a little thick across the middle and needed a shave badly, but was handsome and rugged. She placed him to be late thirties, with good hair and nice teeth and nice arms. No, great arms … like two tan trucks, criss-crossed with veins and ending in large, perfect, ring-less hands.

Elson made for the door. She slowed her pace, swung her hips in an exaggerated saunter. Just outside the door she stopped, fished a cigarette out of her bag and leaned back out of the wind to light it.

It took him longer to approach her than she had antici-pated. He had dark eyes and they were nearly expressionless as he asked her for a light. She handed over the lighter and waited. After a few consolatory puffs he asked her name. She made one up on the spot and flashed a smile.

"Are you going to finish that cigarette before you ask me out?" Elson was delighted to see surprise creep across his features.

"What makes you think I was going to ask you out?" Elson thought that his sudden smile made him very handsome indeed. They stood there, smiling at each other.

"Well, if you weren't, then I certainly apologize. However, if your intention was more than idle chat and a smoke, here is my number and I'm free most nights after 9." Elson handed him the business card she'd plucked from her bag and stepped out and away from him.

"My name is Ryan," he called out after her. Elson thought, *nice name* and then little else.

Ryan, as it turned out, did intend to ask her out and did so that very afternoon. He called a little past four and ten minutes into her last class of the day. She made plans to meet him at a local watering hole downtown, giving herself enough time to run home and change beforehand. She thought he'd cleaned up nicely, having traded in his dusty contractor garb for a clean pair of wide leg jeans and loose sweater with a zippered neck.Elson perched on her bar stool in a thigh-hugging black skirt and strappy, cherry-colored high heels that matched her fitted blouse.

Ryan's eyes dripped down her frame, he smiled at her approvingly. Drinks and dinner passed uneventfully. Ryan proved to be an adequate conversationalist, if a little on the dry side. He was midway through some story about a deck he'd been working on suddenly collapsing, when Elson leaned forward and ran her hand up the inside of his thigh.

"Get the check, Ryan." Then picking up his car keys from the table asked, "What do you drive?"

He took a few moments to collect himself in the face of her behavior. "Dark blue Ford 350," he answered, simultaneously waving the bartender over.

"Of course. That's where I'll be." Elson leaned into his space and briefly touched her lips to his, pulling back before he had a chance to return the kiss.

Ryan still looked strangely startled when he tugged open the door of the pickup a few minutes later. "You don't fuck around do you?" he grinned at her.

Elson slid across the wide leather seat and wrapped her arms around his neck. "No Ryan, that's just the point, I do." "Do what?" he asked, already breathless in the wake of her wet kisses, her hot mouth.

"Fuck around," Elson said, tugging at his belt, pulling him free of his jeans.

Ryan's stunned confusion gave way to a ferocious lust and he tugged her small breasts free from her lace bra, greedily sucking them into his mouth. Elson tugged her skirt up over her hips. She wasn't wearing any panties. With a throaty sigh, she lowered herself onto his shaft. With steering wheel pressing into her back, she rocked back and forth, letting him cup her ass to lift her up and down the length of him. It lasted a few frenzied minutes before he came loudly, howling, biting into her shoulder and squeezing her ass so hard she was sure there would be bruises. This last thought sent her into her rushing into her own climax. The heat rose up inside her and she could almost feel the brittle skin cells expanding, feel the renewal pulsing beneath her skin, coursing through her. She convulsed and shook with her orgasm, her body contracting down on him, squeezing and grinding flesh to flesh.

Spent and a little breathless, she slipped off him and slide down onto her back on the front seat, not bothering to tug her skirt back down over her hips. In the dim light, her pink nipples were high and hard and Ryan could see her sex was shaved clean. Elson arched her back and opened her thighs, giving him an all access show. She reached down and touched herself; her clit was a glistening nub that she rubbed with the tips of her ruby fingernails.

"We aren't done I hope?" she asked, seductively.

"Can I take you home?" he said, salivating over her body like a school boy. He could feel his erection growing rock hard again.

"Why? I like it here, in your big truck." She began to gyrate against his seat, bouncing her ass on the leather and she fingered herself harder.

Ryan knew that they had been lucky here but the longer they stayed, the better chance someone would see them. At least he could drive somewhere close that was a little more private. Elson pouted, but still continued to play with herself on the short drive to the construction site.

It was a modern two story house, little more than walls and a foundation but it was at the end of a cul de sac, in a new development that currently had no occupied residences. He parked around the back of the structure and doused the headlights. He turned back to Elson, who had suddenly sat up and looked around with renewed interest.

"You want to stay in the car? Or get out where we have more room?"

By way of an answer, Elson slipped out of her bra and threw open the door. She looked around in the dark, momentarily confused, until he took her hand and led her through the back door of the house and into a large room that was destined to be the gourmet kitchen. The pieces of the granite countertop stood like silent sentries waiting to be installed. Ryan grabbed Elson around her waist and sat her on the plastic sheeting that covered the closest unit. He pulled her knees apart and buried his head between her thighs.

Elson thought Ryan was much better at using his mouth on her than he was at talking to her. She slipped and slid on the cold plastic as he sucked and licked at her eagerly. She came quickly, her body vibrating against his teeth, her breasts heaving above his head. He wasted no time flipping her around, bending her forward over the counter and plunging inside her. She met each thrust with her hips and ass, slapping back against him with just as much force. Determined to find her deep center, he gripped her hips and drove himself up into her, taking her toes off the ground and nearly driving her over the top of the counter. He reached around and grabbed her breasts, pinching her nipples and biting into her neck. They came together, bucking and moaning, the sounds of their union bouncing off the walls of the hollow house.

Ryan felt depleted, elated and more alive than he had ever felt, but depleted. He looked over at the girl; *she had said her name was Sarah, hadn't she?*

She was in the process of tugging her shirt down over her hips. He admired the curve of her back as she bent to adjust the strap on her heel, the way her perfect tits rushed forward when she bent over. He was recalling how hot and tight her pussy had been when he noticed the first ache in his arm. Before he had a chance to say a word, the same pain became a blinding flash that knocked him off his feet. He had the strange sensation of weightlessness before he lost all feeling below his neck. He rolled terrified eyes toward Elson, making a few soft, guttural noises.

Elson stepped closer, bent down to peer at Ryan, lying helpless on the dirty, unfinished floor. He had not had the chance to zip himself back up and his admirable cock lay flaccid and flopping against his thigh. Deciding, with a monocum of mercy, to save his dignity, Elson expertly tucked it back inside his jeans. She leaned down, cupped one of her breasts and slipped it inside his gaping mouth as he gasped for air. She smiled as she felt him close down on the nipple with his gnashing teeth, his very last defense. The pain ricocheted through her, radiated down her spine and vibrated deep inside her core.

"Go ahead Ryan; bite it off if you'll feel better. I'll just grow a new one," she challenged, but the pressure of the bite was already fading. The great chest stopped heaving. Death always came so quickly for them. Elson was almost envious.

Elson left him, went out and collected her things from the truck. She needn't worry about her DNA or prints; they would never find either in any database anywhere ever. The people that had seen them together at the bar would describe a very different looking woman. Her camouflage was complicated but effective. She looked down at the bruised nipple and areola, the red ring of teeth marks looked like a scar on the creamy skin. It would be gone by morning, along with every tiny wrinkle and frown line, gray hair and liver spot she had found. Age was the only disease she suffered from but she had found the perfect cure for that.

WHAT SUSANNAH DID

Elizabeth Egan

"Bloody batteries!" Susannah roared as she hurled the vibrator across the room.

She groaned and swung her legs over the side of the bed, slouching and sighing till the arousal passed. This part of her life never went right anymore. A walk to the letterbox down the long driveway might dispel the throbbing need. Anything would help. Normally she picked up the mail as she drove in and out of their acreage, but a stroll might take her mind off things. *Maybe.*

The sunshine and fresh air were curative. I really am happy here, she thought after a few deep breaths. I've got the life I always wanted - the well-paid husband, the kids, the country life. The house is ordinary but it's good enough for now. Sure, Aaron's not the most exciting guy I've ever known, certainly not the best in bed, but he loves me, and he's rock solid. I love him too, I guess, but it's not like he's the answer to *all* my prayers.

Susannah smiled at the memory of how bets were laid when she was twenty years old that she wouldn't reach thirty, let alone achieve the dreams she bored her friends with. Unemployed, druggie dropouts from Uni don't kick the habit, get financial, meet a straight guy who's got a life, move to the country and have a family, like normal people. It just doesn't happen, they told her. She laughed out loud at the triumphal fun she would have had collecting on those bets, but most of that crowd was probably dead by now. Nor would they be likely to recognize her: the furtive, shadowed eyes were clear and bright; the lusterless hair was shaped and shining; her long limbs were lithe and strong, instead of scrawny and sallow skinned.

She looked at the neighbor's black and white Holstein dairy cattle placidly grazing and behind them at the paddocks rising to wooded hills that caught low clouds in winter. Their three acres of pasture had been turned to lawn and garden, and every day more types of birds than she ever knew existed came to visit. Pairs of Wood duck pattered along, a flock of cattle herons fanned out across the grass to harvest insects, and the single whistle of a king parrot alerted her to look in the trees for their brilliant red chests. Real top-knot pigeons, huge and plump, with orange neck decorations, arrived from the hills to feed with the wallabies, and red breasted robins and blue-eyed wattle birds visited at different times of year. She had been quite unaware before they moved here that such visual richness could be part of everyday life.

Her group had been totally preoccupied with where their next hit was coming from, and what scam they had to pull to get the money to pay for it. Sometimes they shoplifted or pawned things that fell from the back of trucks. Susannah was scared witless when they burgled. There was always an adrenalin high on those jaunts, but the letdown afterwards, before the relief of the hit, made her feel she had bottomed out, and was stuck there. On rare occasions she had been able to step back and see just how pointless and inwardly focused her life was - so sordid, so … going nowhere.

Heaven help anyone who led her babies down that path. They would be dead meat if she caught them. As she walked, she replayed the morning ritual when she dropped them at school.

"Bye-bye, possums. Have a lovely day and make sure you eat all your lunch."

Emily would hang off the sign that read *Westerly Falls School. Founded 1863* as her mother hoisted the backpack over her shoulders. There was only a lunch box and a warm top inside, but carrying a bag made Emily feel like a big kid. Tom would already be running off for a game with his mates, his bag jolting against skinny legs.

"I love you, Mummy," Emily whispered each day at the last touch of her mother's hand, and Susannah would pat her daughter's face and pucker a kiss, then stand by the car in jeans and tracky top to watch her little girl's blond corkscrew curls bob along the concrete path covered in so many gumnuts, twigs and fallen leaves it looked like a bush track winding under the tall spotted gums.

During the drive back home each day, warm contentment flowed over her. The picturesque countryside was hers to look at any day - lush, bright green kikuyu grass ran all the way to the fringe of trees along the river bank. They had a favorite spot for swimming where the river did a long, lazy loop that left a pebble and sand beach on one side. Someone had climbed a tall tree and tied a rope to make a breathtaking swing for anyone game enough to drag the rope's tail to the top of the bank and launch themselves in a flying lunge out over the shallows to drop off in the deep channel. Boys of the town did it on hot days to astonish onlookers.

Susannah took the mail from the box and started to walk back. She opened mundane items as she went but saved anything interesting till she got to the veranda bench. There was one letter for her marked *Personal* with no return address. The handwriting was shaky and the grubby envelope reminded her of other times. Even seated Susannah shook apprehensively as she opened it. Her eyes dropped immediately to the signature. *Nick.* Shit! Oh shit! Her heart pounded hard enough to burst her chest wide open and leaden flashes filled her head and stomach.

How had he found her? What did he want? In her thrill-seeking days she had been hypnotized by his menacing self-confidence, and perplexed by his unsociable behavior. The slow, purposeful speech was only ever intended to persuade others to meet his needs. He was the most dangerous experience of her life - a satanic, single-facetted James Dean. His

147

stares to her when they first met were so sexually loaded that she had trouble getting past that point. She tried to find something deeper in him, but it was an empty well. He was not a whole person, but he filled a need in her, in a way no one else had ever done. The great sex kept her hooked. There were plenty of others to compare him with, but as time distilled the memory, they fell aside and left Nick as the personification of a tantalizing, earth moving, orgasmic energy.

But that's all there was to Nick. He drifted on the fringe of groups like a rogue wild thing: hostility simmered beneath his sullen exterior and flared to violence with the slightest provocation - he was a vicious brawler. She knew it was flirting with danger to be with him but the sharp edge of risk, and lust, always drew her back. When Susannah felt his flickering malevolence turn on her, she tried to wean herself off him, but she was an insect in his web.

"Come round tonight, Susannah," he would ooze at her. "Don't let me down, sweet thing. I'll be waiting for you."

Sometimes she made herself go out with friends instead, and he did not disappoint her expectations of revenge. The stakes were raised each time they came together after she had avoided him. He was increasingly sadistic and found new ways to administer excruciating droplets of pain. Still, she had to say, the sex was totally mind-blowing. The cruelest times were when he tantalized her to a moaning, sexual delirium before tipping her unceremoniously on the floor, ungratified, shocked and bruised.

"Get out, bitch, and come when I tell you next time," he would say.

He never really agreed to let her go, and laughed when she said she was through with him. Every time she felt she was coming out from under his dark cloud she would get distraught with horniness. Nick knew just how she worked, and after a couple of weeks he would ring to offer a night of fun, just once more, for old time's sake. That's how it went for months. Susannah tried to put more time between each meeting, and as her addiction subsided, he enticed her with veiled threats, but promises, too, that the next time would be the last.

"Come on, babe. I need you here 'cos you're the best. You know you'll love it. Then I'll let you go," he'd say.

Susannah fell for it a few times but always worried she would not escape unscathed. After all, he was mad, she realized that. She never really knew herself whether she went because she was afraid, or for his special brand of satisfaction.

Eight years ago she fled to the country telling no one where she went. It all came back as she sat on the veranda staring at the letter. Elemental fear and primal need surged through her in turn. She replayed her and Nick's movements as if they were an elite sporting combination. They had complemented each other to perfection - meeting late in the evening for a night of tumultuous sex, and parting at dawn, both totally satisfied.

That raunchy, hedonistic, physical stuff was the only thing Susannah missed in her new life. She had convinced herself that she could live without it, but sitting with the hot sun on her inner thigh, and Nick's letter in her hand, she found herself breathing in rhythm to a pulsation in her lower body. Even holding the letter ignited a need she thought was put aside.

The letter was typically Nick: *I know I said I'd let you go, but I can't forget how good we were together. It took me a while to find you, but now I know where you are, I want to see you, I want to fuck you, bitch, the way we used to, just one more time, then I'll leave you alone.*

The endearing, persuasive Nick, all lies and promises. He had not changed. If she saw him and they started up again, she would never be free of him. Maybe she could see him on the side and have the best of both worlds, but if she refused to see him he could make her life miserable. What if he threatened the children? She could not let that happen. She did not want to lose anything in her new life.

But what if …?

* * *

Susannah sent an unsigned letter to Nick that she printed on the computer in the town library.

Meet me outside the post office at Westerly Falls on Wednesday 10th at 10.00am. Get out so I can see it's you. I'll make sure you see me. Don't talk to me, just follow when I leave. There's a hut near an old dairy about twenty minutes away. We'll be alone there. I'll only see you this one time, Nick, then you have to leave me alone. I'm not going back to my old life.

Every thought up till the 10th conflicted with the one before and after it. Part of me really, really wants this, she thought, but what if he hurts me and I can't get help? No one will know where I am. Will this work to get rid of him? What if Aaron finds out? Am I protecting my family or endangering them?

Nick turned up on schedule in the main street of Westerly Falls, elbow out the car window, cruising like a shark. Susannah tried not to look at him and he pulled in behind her at an unobtrusive distance. She barely managed the gears as she led the way out of town, into the hills, past a stretch of forest and out onto some cleared paddocks at the top of a low range where a dairy herd used to graze. They pulled up and got out of their cars. She was excited, fearful, and breathing hard. They circled and stopped a couple of meters apart.

"Nice car. Yours?" she asked.

"Na. Borrowed, prob'ly insured. He'll be right."

"Oh, so nothing's changed."

Susannah lugged a heavy picnic basket inside the cabin. "I thought we might as well do the food and drinks in style, because it sure isn't The Hilton in here." She tried to sound lighthearted.

The dilapidated slab-timber hut had been patched with corrugated iron. The timber floor was beginning to give way. The only furniture was an iron-ended, sagging single bed with a grotty mattress. The brick chimney would stand long after the rest had fallen down.

"Remember this? Your favorite Old Crow bourbon. Coke too, sorry, no ice."

Susannah handed him a large bourbon with a dash of coke. She poured herself a tequila and took a series of quick sips. Nick was not talking. Susannah was just as keen to get down to business, but wanted to make her terms clear.

"We've got all day," she said, "but since this is the only time we'll be seeing each other we might as well make the most of it. We drink some, we eat some, we screw some, then we do it all again. That's the way I want it. Here, drink."

She made him have another stiff one before he touched her. They tried to spin it out but there was no holding back. They had to let go, but it was only the beginning. In the interludes while they recouped energy and appetite Susannah ate a lot and drank a little, Nick drank a lot and Susannah offered him only titbits of food. They feasted of each other in every way, fulfilling every need, desire, whim and fancy. Susannah spent most of the last and longest union propped on her elbows leaning out through the empty window, falling into the landscape with each surge of Nick against and in her from behind. Each rocking, thrusting movement was like the click of a camera imprinting the trees and birds and clouds into her brain. Each flash of scenery would be forever linked with that erotic day.

When they were finished she led him to the bed where they lay together. Normally he would not have cared for that, but exertion and Old Crow had taken its toll.

"That was great, Nick. As good as ever. What a team! I'll remember today always." Before he dropped off to sleep

Susannah told him, "I have to go in a few minutes, I'm expected elsewhere. You stay a bit. We can't be seen going through town at the same time. Just leave when you're ready. No one will ever know we were here. OK?"

Nick grunted. So far, so good. Susannah gathered every scrap she had brought and dallied with her dressing till Nick was sound asleep, then covered him with an old rug. Reaching into the bottom of the basket she took out a large cake tin, then slowly opened the lid at arm's length to make sure the bag inside was done up. She gingerly loosened the ties and emptied the contents under the blanket against Nick. A nice, warm, dark spot.

It had taken all her courage to catch this fellow, a medium size brown. She knew where they lived in a pile of rocks, and had released a box of mice there in the last few days so they would not be ravenous and aggressive, but scooping one into a bag with a loop of wire was something she hoped never to have to do again.

The snake would settle under the covers ... until Nick rolled on it. With several bites, still half-drunk and no idea where he was, especially if it was dark by then... Well, he had given a good farewell performance.

Susannah blew Nick a kiss, plucked her letter from his pocket, picked up the basket and walked out into the sunshine, motherhood and respectability. She sniffed at the warm afternoon sunlight falling softly on the dried grass. Kangaroos looked at her blankly, masticating. Susannah smiled and began to chuckle. The chuckles mounted on each other till she threw back her head and laughed long and hard at the openness above her. Tears ran down her cheeks.

"I beat you, Nick, you prick. I beat you."

WHEN THE VOWEL BREAKS

William Andre Sanders

Lindsey had been suspicious of her husband, Paul, for the past two months.

He'd been acting weird towards her. Emotionally cold, careless and secretive. He was not the same man she married seven years ago. Paul was sensitive and charming back then. Nowadays, however, there was absolutely no warm connection between the two of them. She honestly believed Paul was cheating on her. He had to be.

Lindsey parked across the street from the small brick house on 114 Bell Street. She was supposed to still be at work and not get off until after three more hours, but she pretended to have gotten sick and so the boss let her go early. Nightly business at the diner was slow as usual, anyway. There wasn't anything that the two teen waitresses she worked with, couldn't handle on their own.

Closing the car door as quietly as possible and making her way across the street, Lindsey stared at the silver Mustang parked behind Paul's truck in the driveway.

Someone was clearly keeping him in good company.

She glimpsed at the license plate. Personalized tags: *1HOTFOX.*

1HOTFOX was no stranger to Lindsey. The dirty-blond, blue eyes, perfect tan owner of the silver Mustang was her close friend, Kristen. They'd been good friends for well over fourteen years — spanning all the way back to their days of attending high school together.

Bypassing the Mustang and getting beside the bed of Paul's truck, Lindsey raised the lid on the left side compartment of his toolbox and looked inside. It was entirely pitch-

153

black. She couldn't see anything. She reached one hand down into the toolbox and— *Cling! Clang!* ... was all she heard while hitting together what were apparently wrenches and screwdrivers on the toolbox floor. Then she brushed across something else. A hard plastic case with a push-button on the side. Curiously, she applied pressure to the button.

Clack. Clack. Clack. Clack, it sounded, moving forward.

Lindsey slid the button back down into place, making that same noise all over again.

She withdrew the piece from the toolbox. One brief glance and she knew what it was right away; a utility knife, which was last year's birthday present from her.

Paul Thompson, it is time to show you **WHO** *not to mess with* ... she thought, closing the toolbox and strutting with intent toward the house.

She opened the screen door quietly, then unlocked and opened the wood door in silence. The inside of the house was dark, so dark that Lindsey vaguely outlined the living room furniture. As far as she could see, there wasn't a light turned on anywhere. She did manage, though, to bend around the side of the couch and dodge the lamp and end table beside the recliner, before tiptoeing sneakily down the hallway to the bedroom.

The door was ajar. Dim light bled through the crack and that was about as far as it went. She stood outside the room, listening.

Paul and Kristen were moaning and grunting and pitching sounds people don't make regularly.

"Ah, baby, ride this dick. Oh, yeah," Paul said with difficulty breathing.

Kristen groaned.

Lindsey pushed the door open enough to see them on the bed. Kristen was straddling him and grinding up and down slowly. She arched her back, tilted her head, and sank her fingers into long lengths of hair on the sides of her head.

A surge of instant rage turned Lindsey's face red. She could feel her skin burning as she began to sweat. Gazing onto them with narrowed eyes, she worked the button on the utility knife up and down. Up and down.

Then a peculiar transformation of emotion took her over unexpectedly. She sensed a total loss of being pissed off. She gathered the sense of having warm sticky arousal flow out from between her legs and onto her panties instead. She begun trembling slightly, also, and her breathing was a little more intense. Perhaps she was imagining herself in Kristen's position. Regardless of what had thrown her into a sexual frenzy, Lindsey wanted so badly to experience pleasure she hadn't received for a long while.

She slipped the knife inside the pants pocket of her waitress uniform, and pushed the door open all the way and emerged slowly into the center of the doorway.

Paul noticed her immediately and shoved Kristen off him, landing her beside him on the bed. Then he pulled the bed sheet over his waist and jolted upright. "Uh— ... babe, shit! I mean, before you say anything, first hear me out, please! This is the first time this has happened! Honest to God's truth!"

Lindsey took one step forward. She was silent, thinking about what to say and how to say it. She wasn't ready to allow her voice to bleed seduction. "I know better than to believe you, Paul," she said, putting great effort into sounding harsh. "Feed that shit to someone else. This has been going on for quite a while."

"No it hasn't, really," he said.

Lindsey bit her lip, reserved breath and looked at Kristen.

Kristen seemed not to mind expressing enjoyment for occupying her best friend's man. Entirely naked, firm nipples insinuating her hunger for cock was ongoing; her beauty pageant smile didn't crack the slightest signal of worry or embarrassment. "Don't let him fool you." She spoke in a way as if nothing was the matter.

"What?!" Paul jerked his head around and looked at her. The show of confusion on his face was so convincing that a daytime soap opera star would have a hard time succeeding with better results. "What are you trying to do?!"

Lindsey's quivering lips no longer could suppress her true feelings. She smiled. "It's okay, Paul. I've known for a long while the things you've been doing behind my back."

He looked at Lindsey, still puzzled. "I don't know what you're talking about!"

Kristen pressed a hand on his chest. "Be honest with her, honey. She is your wife." She brushed the tip of her finger down the center of his stomach. "Tell her how many times you begged for some pussy."

He smacked her hand away instantly. "You're fucking crazy! Get the hell off me!"

Lindsey unbuttoned her pants and slowly slipped out of them. "Did you really think that I wouldn't know?"

Paul didn't say anything. The long expression on his face suggested that he'd fallen disoriented by the ordeal of watching his wife strip, with him in bed with another woman.

Kristen giggled. "Damn girl. I always knew you had some freak in you, but I never once thought that it'd be off the chain."

Lindsey kicked the work pants beside the bed and pulled her shirt up and over her head.

Finally, Paul said dumbly, "Are you serious?"

Standing in a matching pair of bra and panties, Lindsey dropped the shirt on the floor and shrugged her shoulders. "Why not? I'm the reason you're fucking her in the first place. I put Kristen up to seducing you months ago – to find out if you are as true to me as you claim."

Kristen leaned toward him, planting her hand on top of the sheet between his legs. She wasn't touching him but she was close. "She is telling the truth. All of this was put together by her."

"You're crazy," Paul stated with disbelief.

"And now, here I am. Wanting to get a little action of my own, and you have a problem with it," Lindsey said.

"No!" He replied quickly.

"Okay, then what is the problem?"

Brows raised and eyes stretched wide-open, he confessed. "Nothing is wrong. I've wanted for us to be able to get involved in something like this. I think it would help ignite a spark in our love life and make things interesting again."

Lindsey closed her mouth. She had nothing more to add to the conversation.

Paul didn't mention another word either. Based on her silence, he assumed that his desire to participate in a threesome was the wrong secret to let her in on.

Kristen was quiet too.

Wandering to the side of the room, Lindsey stood in front of the chest of drawers. She opened the top drawer. The one that her and Paul referred to as the *Naughty Box*. And it was naughty. She pulled from the drawer a black blindfold, two handcuffs, and a purple vibrating dildo—roughly seven inches long.

"That isn't coming anywhere near me!" Paul squalled.

Lindsey laughed, slamming the drawer shut. "This isn't for you, silly."

Kristen shivered excitedly. "Damn well better be for me."

Lindsey dropped the dildo and the blindfold onto the bed, then tossed a pair of handcuffs over to Kristen. "You get that hand and I'll get this one."

Paul raised his arms in front of the metal bar across the headboard and allowed both women—at exactly the same time—to secure the cuffs to the bed rail and restrain his wrists. He yelped and jerked his arm. "Dammit! Be easy!"

Lindsey had obviously tightened the cuff a lot more than Kristen did around his opposite wrist. She picked up the blindfold and threw it on his chest, then looked at Kristen.

"Put that on him."

"Hold on a minute," Paul insisted. "Do I not get to watch the two of you do a little something with each other?"

Lindsey sighed and rolled her eyes at him. "You're so typical."

"Come on," he begged, "I've been waiting for this."

"No," she said mirthfully.

"At least let me see the—"

"Cover his eyes, Kristen," she cut in.

Kristen put the blindfold on his face and pulled its strap over the back of his head. "Don't worry about what you can't see. Just use your imagination. You might actually like it better this way," she said, tugging the blindfold down on top of his eyes.

"Oh, he is gonna squirm to no end after he finds out what I have in store for him," Lindsey guaranteed.

She moved to the foot of the bed and reached behind herself and undid her bra. "Give me your bra" she said, uncovering her ripe little A-cup titties.

"Why?"

Lindsey wrapped the bra cups firmly around his left ankle and crossed one bra strap over and the other bra strap under the bed rail in front of him, tying them tightly to the frame. "You have to get creative when there aren't any more cuffs to go around."

"Wow. I never would have once thought about doing something like that."

"Get your bra," Lindsey snapped.

Kristen literally jumped on her command.

Paul pressed the pillow, and wiggled his arms up and down along the headboard. "Come on. Don't keep me waiting any longer."

Kristen leaned over the side of the bed, swooped down with one hand, grabbed the bra, and tossed it to Lindsey. Quickly, Lindsey wrapped it around his other ankle and tied it to the bed rail. She pulled the bra and then yanked the other one. They were as tight as she could make them. "That should do it," she said.

Kristen giggled briefly, "Oooh, Lindsey … kinky girl."

Lindsey grinned, looking on the bed while reaching for the dildo. "You've known me to have a couple of wild moments."

"None of which I've seen," Paul uttered blandly.

"Hush," Kristen slapped the side of his leg, "you're gonna ruin the moment."

Lindsey picked the purple seven-inch monster off the bed and aimed its fat head straight at Kristen's face. With her quietest voice she said, "Let's show him what we're all about."

Kristen positioned herself on her hands and knees with Paul's legs between them. Her head lolled above his waist. She grasped the sheet draped over him and glimpsed back at Lindsey.

"Stick it to me," she said, naughtily.

Lindsey smirked. "I'm gonna stick it to you like it's never been stuck."

Kristen groaned with passionate anticipation. "Be rough. Fuck me hard," she said, heatedly.

Lindsey smacked her tan ass before gripping her hip and slipping the head of the dildo between the gaping bald lips on her vagina. She pushed the rubber shaft inside her halfway, then pulled it almost completely out of her. Kristen moaned. Lindsey thrust forward again. In and out.

In and out.

All of a sudden Kristen became quiet and jerked the sheet away from Paul's mid-section. The tip of his firm penis stood just inches from brushing across her nose. It was so close to her that she smelled the fruity aroma her pussy had left on him recently. She opened her mouth—closing her eyes and bowing her head—and wrapped her lips around the slick head of his dick.

Lindsey watched in disgust. She became so disgusted by

watching that she lost the rhythm to what she was doing, and began jabbing the dildo deep inside of her. *Very quickly.*

Nevertheless, Kristen gave very little response to the rapist-style aggression striking violently between her legs. The most sound Lindsey heard come out of her was a mild *ugh* here, and a vague *ugh* there. It seemed obvious that Kristen had lost interest in her and was concentrating hard on delighting Paul.

"Yeah, baby, do it like that. Don't stop," Paul said satisfyingly.

As far back as Lindsey could remember, she'd never heard Paul talk that way to her. She reflected on her and Kristen's private relationship. They weren't only the best of friends, they were lovers, too. Both knew what to do to bring the other to orgasm, and knew exactly when to do it. Although it didn't appear to be true at the moment, Kristen told Lindsey—a long time ago—that she was the best thing that had ever happened to her. *Nonsense.* Lindsey might have believed it then, but she sure as hell didn't take it into consideration now. Kristen had never moaned so gratifyingly during all the intimate moments that they had shared.

Lindsey leaned over the side of the bed and reached towards the floor, withdrawing the slippery warm dildo from the thick lips of Kristen's vagina.

Click. Click. Click.

She set the dildo on the bed and raised the utility knife to her side. The retractable blade was extended. She assumed that neither Kristen nor Paul heard the blade push forward, because Paul kept breathing heavily while grunting as though he was about to cum, and Kristen maintained a steady pace of rocking her head up and down on top of him. All of a sudden Lindsey grabbed a handful of hair and jerked her off Paul and pulled her straight up against her. With her breasts pressing Kristen's back, they stood upright on their knees.

Kristen snarled and hissed. "Ouch! Not that hard!" she

yelped.

"Hey. What's going on? Why did you stop?" Paul asked.

Lindsey yanked the fistful of hair causing Kristen to tilt her head farther backwards. "Sounds to me like you've developed a strong taste for prick," Lindsey said unhappily, "bet you can't get enough, can you?"

Kristen reached both hands behind her head and fought to free herself from the harsh grip Lindsey had on her. "Let go! You're hurting me!"

Lindsey shoved her head forward and then pulled it back again, violently.

Kristen winced and shrieked.

Lindsey pressed her cheek on the side of Kristen's head. "Come on, Kristen … tell me the truth. Did you get off on the feeling of having your cunt filled with dick?"

"Yes! Yes! But only because it's different compared to what we do!"

Lindsey frowned. "I expected you'd say that."

"Don't take it the wro-"

Lindsey let go of her hair and covered her mouth. "We would've been perfectly compatible had you not taken things this far."

"Okay, that's enough! Cut out the chic-chat!" Paul suggested frustratingly.

Kristen reached up to pull Lindsey's hand away from her mouth—when Lindsey raised the utility knife and scraped the blade across her throat. Blood poured out of her neck instantly, and flowed down over her chest and stomach just as quickly as it had leaked out while the cut was being made.

Kristen let out a muffled scream. She gagged, then became deathly silent. Her shoulders slouched and her arms dropped to her sides with total relaxation. The moment Lindsey withdrew from covering her mouth, Kirsten's head drooped forward and rocked to either side without any control. Clearly, she was dead.

Lindsey let go and the still bleeding body fell over sideways on the bed. She looked at Paul.

His erection was dying, also.

She crawled close to him, reaching down and grabbing the partially soft shaft glazed with Kristen's saliva. She stroked up and down slowly, making him hard again.

"Feels good," he said, taking in a difficult breath.

"You like that?" she asked lovingly.

"Ah, yeah. Keep on going, like that."

She did slightly enjoy pleasuring him, however, busting his nut was no where near what she had in mind to achieve.

"You're doing great, baby," he said.

She groped him several more times before stopping at the top of the shaft, squeezing so hard that the head of his penis turned blood red.

Paul wailed in opposition of pleasure. "What the hell are you doing?!"

Lindsey placed the knife blade beside his dick but held back from touching him with it. She looked at his blindfolded face. "Do you honestly think that I would let you get by with sticking your dick in places it has no business going?"

"I thought you said this is what you wanted!"

"In case you haven't noticed, Paul, dear, our marriage is in complete ruins. There is nothing that can repair the extent of damage that has been done to us up to this point. Absolutely nothing. Zero. And this," she laughed wildly, "this is over-the-fucking-top. You're always finding some way to disgust me."

"You are outta your goddam mind!" He shook his arms—rattling the handcuffs aggressively—and struggled with exceptional effort just to move his legs. "Get all this shit off me right now!"

Lindsey rubbed the blade on the side of his penis. He squalled immediately. She moved the blade directly beneath the gash after realizing that she'd drawn blood.

"What the fuck—you stupid bitch! What are you doing to

me?!"

"What I should have done to you years ago," she said calmly. "Make you think of me when considering who to fuck next and working yourself up to a hard-on."

"You're being ridiculous. I haven't messed around with—"

"Liar!" Lindsey preformed another abrasion on his bloody penis. "Liar! Liar! Liar!"

Paul screamed. The pitch of unbearable pain penetrated her ears with such horror to guarantee a lifetime of haunting memories.

She completed three slits on the side of his penis, and then moved the knife to the other side. The cuts reminded her of gills on a fish, a mangled fish, bleeding badly after getting butchered on the cutting block, in a chef's kitchen. Blood was everywhere, on Paul's hips and thighs, on the bed between his legs. Lindsey's hands were covered with crimson; several large dabs of warm scarlet had spewed onto her body.

Paul cried loudly. Eventually, he lessened to making only quiet whimpering sounds. He was losing so much blood, his erection withered away quickly.

She retracted the blade and dropped the knife onto the bed. She glanced over to the bed sheet and blanket heavily saturated with blood, glimpsing across Kristen's body, and then looked back down at Paul. Strangely, she didn't feel remorse for her actions. No regret. All she sensed was having the heavy weight of burden lifted out of her.

Paul's breathing hit the downward spiral. His chest hardly rose during each difficult inhalation of sexually rancid air. He was trembling constantly, in pain and shock.

She knew it was only a matter of minutes before he wouldn't be moving or breathing, he was still losing a substantial amount of blood. Based on how much he'd lost already, it appeared that luck was the only thing keeping him alive.

She stood from the bed slowly and turned her back to the

gory aftermath of her rage. Without speaking another word to Paul, she slipped out of the room, making her way to the bathroom.

Lindsey flipped the light on. In the large mirror above the black marble sink she saw her bloody reflection looking back at her. For a moment she got lost in a mess of sprinkled crimson dots.

But then—

She wasn't really thinking about anything when the haunting moan of Kristen's prior enjoyment began pouring out from inside of her head. Then she visualized what she had seen upon arriving outside the bedroom door. The way Kristen had sat on top of Paul and motioned herself gently up and down. How she arched her head back, opening her mouth and rolling her eyes with exhilarating pleasure.

Tears gathered in her earthy green eyes. Seeing it all happen had been torturous enough. Having to go through the experience again—in slow motion and with vivid detail—was punishment by God.

Lindsey closed her eyes. Hoped darkness would be her escape. Instead, memory served another scene. Another moment she wished could be forgotten. Lindsey saw herself positioned behind Kristen and watching everything in front of her move unnaturally slow. Most movement came from Kristen swaying hear head up and down. The slurping and sucking sounds that Kristen was making was deafening in her ears. Then Kristen groaned. The noise dragged out and sounded twice more erotic than when the actual moment took place.

Lindsey opened her eyes again. A couple of tears ran down her face. She couldn't handle knowing Kristen had enjoyed each second of sweating it out with Paul. That wasn't the plan. The plan was for Kristen to seduce him just long enough for her to have good reason to file for divorce. She didn't know why she allowed it to continue for several months. Maybe the fact that Kristen was pregnant with his child—which he knew nothing about—was the reason she didn't react sooner. Her lover impregnated by her husband. It was an outright abnormal circumstance.

Thinking it over made her sick in the stomach. It had been Kristen's idea for her to get a divorce. She wanted to milk Paul for every dollar she could get in child support.

Lindsey didn't see it the same way. Paul was currently her husband and he would be in her life again as the father to her and Kristen's child. She didn't want that. And she knew exactly what she had to do to get him out of the picture completely.

As far as she was concerned, Kristen never should have let herself get pregnant. She should not have revealed vivid luxuriating in taking advantage of the situation either.

Lindsey looked in the mirror. She wondered what went wrong. And how. What troubled her most was thinking about why Kristen showed more satisfaction with Paul than any amount she ever received from her. Had Kristen changed her mind about wanting to be with her? Did Paul miraculously convince her that there was more to him than being a wife-beating bastard and pervert?

No. The idea was ridiculous. Paul didn't have a charming bone in his body. Based on her experience, sex wasn't anything to brag about either. There was nothing special about him. He was just Paul. Yes. A prick.

A man.

She stepped away from the mirror, and climbed inside the bathtub, turning the hot water on before sitting down. A moment or two later, warm water covered her legs and continued rising. She rinsed her arms, breasts, working her way up to her neck and face. Then she took the white bar of soap and rubbed it over her chest.

The water wasn't clear anymore; it had turned pink from the mix of soap and blood.

She slid down with only her head above water, letting go

of the soap and raising both arms stretching them down on the sides of the tub. She leaned the back of her head against the wall. She closed her eyes. The homicidal event repeated in her mind, all the agonizing pain flooding out of Paul's voice, his and Kristen's blood shed carelessly on the bed.

It all played out so clearly as if she had just committed the murders and was still on the bed with their bodies.

Immediately preceding the violent recollection, she heard faint noises coming from someplace close to her in the bathroom; she swore to herself that she'd heard something.

She did.

The sounds made their presence known again. This time louder. Moaning and groaning. They were a passionate combination. Although the voice lacked expressing words, she distinctly recognized that it belonged to Kristen. The powerful moans and groans escalated to sounding the way they did when Paul was thrusting himself inside Kristen.

Lindsey strained her already shut eyes, trying to keep the haunting noises from shattering her sanity. Despite her effort, the sound chiseled its way deep inside her head. It was all she could hear, all that she could think about. And it was all that she could feel flowing throughout her body. Lindsey sank her head slowly beneath the water and held her breath. The moaning and groaning stayed with her, roaring as loudly in water as it had done all around the bathroom.

Suddenly the grim vocal remains of passionate lovemaking drove Lindsey to open her mouth. Her watered down scream sent air bubbles bursting on the surface of pink bath water. She gripped the sides of the bathtub and pushed down to keep herself from jolting upright out of the water. Both legs came up and went down again, splashing water while kicking the inside of the tub. The moaning and groaning were louder than all of the sounds she was making.

Then, at last, her entire body began to jerk aggressively beneath the water, slinging waves over the sides of the bathtub and onto the floor. Her arms trembled restlessly, as well, but she didn't let go of her firm hold on the tub.

Kristen's voice weakened gradually.

And Lindsey stopped stirring under water all at once. She let go of the sides of the tub and her arms went down crashing into the water.

Lustful moans and pleasured groans no longer swirled in the murk of blood and soap around her.

She couldn't hear them anymore, at least.

Long silence —

Love conquered all.

ABOUT THE AUTHORS

Matt Kurtz is a lover of all things horror. When not writing twisted tales, he enjoys watching a frightening flick or reading a terrifying tome. His fiction can be found in anthologies from Evil Jester Press, Pill Hill Press, Blood Bound Books, Comet Press and *Necrotic Tissue* Magazine.

Nelia Thompson has been happily married for over 10 years and believes life should be fun and lived with passion. Her work has previously appeared on Justus Roux's Erotic Tales website and in two anthologies from Living Dead Press.

Anna M. Lowther is an eclectic writer and editor who resides in Ohio with her writer-husband and daughter. Her work has appeared in numerous horror fantasy anthologies and magazines such as Damned in Dixie, Abominations, Black Dragon - White Dragon, Sinister Tales, Theaker's Quarterly Fiction, Necrotic Tissue, Dead Souls, The Scroll of Anubis, and SNM Horrorzine. For more information see *annamlowther@blogspot.com*

Ramon Mendez Jr. is a former Queensborough Community College student currently residing in New York City. He fancies greatly tales of the fantastic, horror and mind numbing suspense and hopes to soon finish his first novel. His work has also been featured in Across Cultures 'A Reader for Writers 8th edition'.

This is **Nathan Robinson's** second story published by Rainstorm Press, his other tale ' Thy Kingdom Come' can be found in Thirsty are the Damned. So far he's had seven monthly winners on www.spinetinglers.co.uk, six stories published by Static Movement, and two more by Thadd Presley Presents . . . His crime thriller 'Top of the Heap was adapted into a podcast by www.pseudopod.org and welcomed rave reviews. Keep up to date with his latest releases at www.facebook.com/NathanRobinsonWrites.

Paul Edmonds lives in Massachusetts. He enjoys writing, music, and the unhealthy study of that old Rod Stewart myth. His recent credits include fiction in Big Pulp and Midnight Screaming.

Douglas Payne is a writer and poet living in Lemon Grove, CA. His work has appeared in Breadcrumb Scabs, Mastodon Dentist, and Vol. 5 of A Year in Ink, an annual anthology of local San Diego writers.

Carol Ann has been writing poetry as long as she can remember; only recently has she begun delving into the depths of story telling in prose form. A 2010 graduate of Grossmont Community College in El Cajon, CA with an AA in English and an AA in Creative Writing she plans to continue her literary education, experience as much of life as possible, and ever endeavor to hone her craft. Her literary and art work has been published in the 2009, 2010, and 2011 editions of Grossmont's literary journal, The Acorn Review.

Michael Matheson is a full time writer, freelance editor, and sometime lecturer. A submissions editor with *Apex*, a book reviewer for *ChiZine*, and the editor of the Friends of the Merril Collection outreach publication *Sol Rising*, he has fiction published or forthcoming in several venues, including *Aoife's Kiss*, the *Lovecraft eZine* and Innsmouth Free Press' *Future Lovecraft* anthology. He maintains an online presence at his blog: A Dark and Terrible Beauty (michaelmatheson.wordpress.com).

Trey Dowell lives in Saint Louis, Missouri with his Anatolian Shepherd proofreader, Lulu. *Safe Sex* was inspired by an encounter with a woman who thought it was "hilarious" to loom over and watch him sleep. It wasn't. Trey has won First Prize honors in Writersweekly.com's 24-hour short story contest, as well as been a finalist in the Writer's Digest Annual Genre Fiction competition. His short story *Ballistic*, published by Untreed Reads, is available in e-book format at all the usual places. His debut novel , *The Aphrodite Way*, will be finished in Spring 2012. If you enjoyed *Safe Sex*, let him know: treyd@swbell.net.

MD Maurice has passionately pursued writing since the six grade. She has been a fan of erotic ever since her first publishing success in

Bare Back Magazine in 2009 and loves the freedom and diversity of the genre. She lives in southeastern New England with her husband and young daughter where she writes as much as humanly possible with a growing toddler in the house.

Elizabeth Egan has worked in tertiary education administration, as a secondary school teacher, in local government and the disability sector. Her qualifications include a Master of Arts (English and Australian Literature) and a Diploma of Education. She currently runs a small grazing property fattening steers. Reading and writing have long been favored hobbies but she also enjoys playing tennis, gardening, spending time with family and traveling. Elizabeth self-published a novel in 2011 (*Sun on Distant Hills*) and is working on a second novel. She writes short stories when inspiration strikes, and has fun writing and attending readings of bush poetry.

William Andre Sanders lives in Narrows, Virginia, with his wife and two children. He is known very little for writing fiction. Even so his dark and always violent imagination has spent the past four years turning out poetry that has appeared in numerous magazines and anthologies. His poem "Raggedy Hag," was printed in *House Of Horror: Best of 2010 Anthology*. In 2005, his psychological horror short story "Eyesight of Insanity," was published in *Seasons In The Night* magazine. The story that you are about to read is Andre's second effort to break into the horror fiction market. And he has penned six more tales upon completion of the following story. None of which have been published ... yet.

ABOUT THE EDITORS

Charlotte Emma Gledson currently resides in the south-coastal town of Gosport, UK. With over 30 stories and poems published in anthologies and magazines, including articles for the 'The Serial Killer Magazine', Charlotte is also penning a supernatural novel entitled, 'Bluebells for my Baby'. Her collection of unsettling stories, 'The Lonely Tree and Other Twisted Tales of Torment' is available at all good book retailers. Recently Charlotte has been posted poetry editor for Dopamalovi Books. Married with four gregarious children and a collection of ventriloquist dummies and porcelain dolls, she finds time relaxing while sipping wine, singing Karaoke and going on paranormal investigations.

Contact her at charlotte@gledson.co.uk or for more information: www.charlottemmagledson.com

Lyle Perez-Tinics (Writer/Editor/Publisher) is the creator of http://www.UndeadintheHead.com a website dedicated to zombie books and the authors. He is the owner & Editor-in-Chief of Rainstorm Press (www.RainstormPress.com) and The Mad Formatter (www.TheMadFormatter.com) a book interior design business. He has stories in many anthologies and is currently working on two novels, *Existing Dead* and *Rising from the Tempest.* He is the mastermind behind *The Undead That Saved Christmas* charity anthology series. He also writes middle grade chapter books under his pen name, Benny Alano. www.BennyAlano.com

Twitter - @LylePerez @RainstormPress @UndeadintheHead
@BennyAlano
www.Facebook.com/RainstormPress
www.Facebook.com/UndeadintheHead

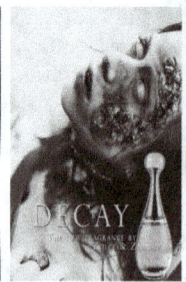

STORY COPYRIGHTS

www.ingramcontent.com/pod-product-compliance
Lightning Source LLC
Chambersburg PA
CBHW070030260626
47159CB00005B/2005